DYING

T0155035

OTHER WORKS BY RENÉ BELLETTO
IN ENGLISH TRANSLATION

Eclipse
Machine

DYING

RENÉ BELLETTO

Translated by Alexander Hertich

Dalkey Archive Press
Champaign and London

Originally published in French as *Mourir* by P.O.L éditeur, 2002
Copyright © 2002 by René Belletto
Translation and introduction copyright © 2010 by Alexander Hertich
First edition, 2010
All rights reserved

Library of Congress Cataloging-in-Publication Data

Belletto, René.
 [Mourir. English]
 Dying / René Belletto ; translated [from the French] by Alexander Hertich.
-- 1st ed.
    p. cm.
 Originally published in French as Mourir, 2002.
 ISBN 978-1-56478-593-0 (pbk. : alk. paper)
 I. Hertich, Alexander. II. Title.
 PQ2662.E4537M6813 2010
 843'.914--dc22
                        2010017537

Partially funded by the University of Illinois at Urbana-Champaign and by a
grant from the Illinois Arts Council, a state agency

Traduit avec le concours du Ministère français de la Culture – Centre national
du Livre

Translated with the support of the French Ministry of Culture – Centre national
du Livre

www.dalkeyarchive.com

Cover: design and composition by Danielle Dutton, illustration by Nicholas Motte
Printed on permanent/durable acid-free paper and bound in the United States
of America

TRANSLATOR'S INTRODUCTION

When writing his novels, René Belletto frequently finds inspiration in other works of art—usually a musical composition or a painting—whose presence informs his books' content and style both. In an interview with the French literary magazine *Lire*, Belletto explained that while composing *Dying* he was constantly drawn towards Diego Velázquez's famous seventeenth-century painting *Las Meninas*, a depiction of the Spanish court under King Philip IV. What propels this work beyond the scope of typical court paintings is the hole at its center. On the left side of the painting is the back of another canvas. The artist, Velázquez, has stepped away for a moment from his work to contemplate his subject, as have the Infanta, the dwarf, and the courtier in the middle ground. The object of their gaze is the subject of much discussion: it could be the viewer, or it could be the royal couple whose reflection one can perceive in a mirror at the far end of the room. The painting is thus enigmatic and complex, playing with multiple perspectives, none of which seems to obviate the others.

While Velázquez is mentioned twice in *Dying*, these passages do not seem central to the text. Yet the original French-language version of *Dying* includes several illustrations, one of which is a reproduction of the celebrated painting. Belletto appears to be inviting us to look upon the painting itself, rather than its subject matter: it is Velázquez's imagery and play with perspective that influenced *Dying*. Filled with mirror images of uncertain worlds, the novel echoes Michel Foucault's famed description of *Las Meninas* in *The Order of Things*: "no gaze is stable . . . subject and object, the spectator and the model, reverse their roles to infinity." Indeed, in its exploration of death and dying, Belletto's novel offers us numerous doubles—duplicate manuscripts, doppelgängers, dreams that echo reality and vice versa—but also lyrics and scores from real and imagined composers, excerpts from other authors—including Belletto—and a mysterious red notebook that seems to already contain the narrators' own tales.

Belletto's own games with perspective make translating and reading *Dying* a tricky business. For both reader and translator, consuming a text is an attempt to understand it, to know it, to classify it—to identify what has happened, in the text, and what has not. *Dying* makes this a perilous process, for Belletto's erudite and writerly work is reminiscent of three other great *B*s in modern fiction: Borges, Beckett, and Blanchot. Perhaps his own "three angels"? Suffice it to say, this text is slippery. Each time we believe we have come to grips with something—the role of a character, the origin of an idea—it seems to crumble between our fingers.

This effect is created through the repetition of words ("a thousand" or "outlaw" (the latter of which is also the title of a novel Belletto published in 2010)), phrases ("between fabric and flesh"), and objects (the red notebook, the baldachin-style four-poster bed), which reappear throughout *Dying* in similar and dissimilar contexts. I have tried to remain as close to the original as possible, so that these very conscious and sometimes subtle uroboric reverberations ring clear. Further obfuscating easy interpretation is the use of multiple narrators. Sixtus, whose overwrought prose anchors the book's first section ("An Old Testament"), may only be part of an allegory invented by the unnamed sculptor who narrates the novel's second section ("A New Testament"), in styles varying from comic dreamscape (the description of his dinner in "The Narvaez Report") to surrealist academic (his philological study of the word prison, "Prizõ"). Yet both authors may simply have copied what they found in the red notebook—whose contents may or may not even be legible—right back into the notebook itself.

And, indeed, some of the book is copied. We find unattributed quotations from the work of composer Clément Janequin and from François Rabelais' *Gargantua and Pantagruel*, both in their original, Renaissance-style Middle French, including knotted syntax and outdated spellings. Even more perplexing are a number of sentences and even page-long excerpts taken directly from Belletto's earlier works, especially his 1986 novel *L'Enfer* ("Hell," translated as *Eclipse*). Like the first section of *Dying*, one of *L'Enfer*'s plotlines tells of a protagonist who finds a large sum of cash and falls in love with a beautiful but troubled woman. Moreover, all of the quotations from *L'Enfer* except for one are found within the "Old Testament" section of the novel. Since the Old Testament is potentially a reimagining of the New, this further refracts our understanding. The notebook and its contents seem to be both subject and object, source and result. How far is hell from dying?

Another of the possible writers of the story we are reading (or a version thereof) is the fictional Spanish composer Miguel Padilla; there is even an autographed picture of him included in the original novel. Yet looking at this photograph, one soon realizes that the individual closely resembles Belletto himself. Is this another wink by Belletto at Velázquez? Similarly, there is a photograph of Queene, who, if we are to believe the narrator of "A New Testament," is only a fictional character. Yves Somme, for whom the narrator initially writes the first part of *Dying*, is also depicted—but this is in fact a drawing of Charles Dickens by Samuel Lawrence. This choice is not insignificant for Belletto. He spent three years writing a 655-page study on Dickens, which his French editor feared would engulf him forever. Has he yet managed to free himself? In this way, photographs and illustrations, which are commonly used mimetically to support arguments and to document the veracity of their claims—"Every photograph is a certificate of presence," Roland Barthes wrote—lose their center. They seem to represent that which is not true.

This is also the case for the use of music and place in the novel. "Bonita," a work for classical guitar by Padilla, is also included among the French-language text's illustrations. But as he is a fictional composer, the composition, while real, is not his. Padilla's works are also featured in the novel's first section, when Sixtus and Queene attend a concert. Initially the orchestra refuses to play, but eventually, through a series of odd coincidences, "the final chord bloomed with such concision that it seemed the obvious finale to a proper performance of the work, which all of us would have then sworn we had attended." Similarly, the hamlet of Couty, home of Sylvie Daumal, does not exist, but the rue Charles Robin in Villeurbanne near Lyon does. There is a small map of the area included in the original edition of *Dying*, yet the description of the street is so hallucinatory—nines become sixes, the narrator sees his double—that one must question its existence.

Just as Velázquez's painting is an exploration of the distance between the perceived and the seen, René Belletto's *Dying* attempts to articulate death, a concept that is ultimately unknowable. With wordplay and shifting perspectives, Belletto pulls us into his novelistic space, where we may hope to tease out meaning, just as the painter's gaze in *Las Meninas* invites us into the pictorial space. But, ultimately, through its multiple reflections, there is no precise answer, no dominant discourse. At the novel's conclusion it is we the readers who enter the building that the narrator has left. The tale and all its uncertainty continues to haunt us, as does death.

ALEXANDER HERTICH, 2010

PART ONE
AN OLD TESTAMENT

I

OBLIVION

SIXTUS *or* THE FIRST SENTENCE

A thousand first sentences, if not to say all, rush to my quill with a howl of collective suicide.

This early spring, believe me, was colder than the cold of winter.

The three squat floors of the Rats and Vermin Hotel were rotting away, piled up at the end of a cul-de-sac in the twelfth arrondissement of the city.

It was here that I was dying.

Not living had taken its toll. The bloom had lost its rose.

I couldn't remember life before the hotel. I had forgotten. Was it that I had seen so little of the world that I no longer remembered it, or had the world so completely deadened me that I could have forgotten?

I didn't know.

Occasionally, roaming the hallways at night, tormented by insomnia, I'd catch a glimpse of a wisp of fabric disappearing around a corner. I'd hurry: it was only Luc, Luc M., the owner, he too was wandering with his monstrous gait through the narrow hallways, filthy and poorly lit, of his cursed establishment. Hey, Sixtus! How's Sixtus? he would ask. Oh, just as you see, I'd say to him. And Luc, how's he? Oh, same as always, pushing up daisies! he would respond, with a grimace drowning in a spatter of spittle, which was his way of signifying mirth.

I didn't know how to respond. But in fact his joking seemed expressly designed to silence you, dominate you, mortify you, annihilate you. Left with your silence, he would press his advantage. He claimed, for example, to have been a war photographer (he photographed me a few times with an ancient camera, which in my opinion had no film in it, just for the pleasure of hearing the click, and what's more I never saw any of his pictures), or to have run a convalescent home for the mortally ill, a clinic called . . . ah yes, the Daisy Pushers! (Again a grimace and a spatter of spittle.) He'd tirelessly tell me about his various lives. I always regretted listening to him. I thought myself weak. But in my defense it must be said that he was my only companion during the interminable duration of my stay at the hotel.

Fine. In the spirit of reconciliation, in order to avoid quarreling, to maintain some semblance of open and equal exchange, I pretended to believe him. I'd tell him that he was lucky to remember things, that I was constantly fighting my poor memory, such as whether or not my father had been a member of POUM, the Spanish anarchist party. But Luc didn't take this well. He thought I was mimicking him, that I was fighting back, that I was playing with words to mock him. "POUM?" he would scornfully repeat, "POUM! Well, after the Daisy Pushers I opened a medical lab, the VIRUM, and then I started a pharmaceutical company that specialized in nasal deturgescents, called SNOT. Absolutely: I founded SNOT!" And then he'd run off, shedding tears of unhappy laughter (and desnotting his nose in the process), his torso shaken by a combination of cachinnation and despair, his hands over his ears so as to be sure he wouldn't hear anything else, and would therefore have the last word.

A child who wanted to be interesting, a pathetic child, even though he was a hundred times older than I.

Or maybe, suddenly changing his tone as well as the subject, and alluding to my nocturnal presence in the hallways, he'd say, "Cheer up, Sixtus! There's nothing like a nice long night of insomnia following an angst-ridden day to make you stare ever more despairingly at an ever-more-hopeless horizon! As for your morning coffee, I should warn you that we're going to have to forgo it. There's a problem with the supplier, etc."

The monster!

AN UNPARALLELED MUSICIAN

One thing, however, was undoubtedly true in the flood of words that I had to endure: although I'd never heard or seen a violin at the hotel, this individual, who feared neither God nor man, had been a child prodigy. But, from the age of sixteen, his doctors had forbidden him to practice his art. Why? Because he played with too much passion, even rage. He put too much of himself into his playing. He had nervous breakdowns. There was no telling what might happen to him. On stage, you couldn't tell the player from the instrument, and some nights it seemed like surgery would be necessary to separate his violin from him.

He then studied medicine and pharmaceuticals. At least that's what he claimed.

THE UNEARTHED MANUSCRIPT

But I must interrupt this first part of my narrative in order to clarify something that I possibly should have announced at the outset: what you are reading is a word-for-word reproduction of a manuscript that I discovered and concealed in a chest of drawers in the lovely house that I later rented with Queene in Madrid. We were able to grant ourselves this little luxury thanks to some of the money that was intended for Armelle M.'s kidnappers, and . . .

But let's wait.

II

FAREWELL

I'll never be able to explain the extreme, fundamental point of conclusion I had reached—but I had reached it. Bravo, Sixtus, hats off, take a bow, I'd say to myself, so true it is that we are always the stubborn authors of our own misfortune, the sly igniters of our own pyre, the indefatigable soilers of our own boots (at the hotel, recently, boots have disappeared), bravo, hats off, head bowed to the ground, head knocking repeatedly against the ground: he's dead, Sixtus, but from what, eh? Well, see, he cracked his skull open against the ground in a burst of admiration for the way he'd reached a point of fundamental conclusion, at the Rats and Vermin Hotel, where he had buried himself alive, poor, malnourished, insomniac, hopeless, condemned!

It happens that one thinks one can discern something stirring inside that might be one's own: it happened that I found the idea of leaving the hotel germinating inside me. I exit, I walk straight ahead, I end up finding a rooming house free of any occupants (in fact, it's off-season), I break in, I get settled, and I answer my door to no one. They knock on my door, they yell, they ring the bell, sound the horn, fire the cannon, all in vain. Open up, Sixtus! Is it possible you don't hear us? Quite possible. Not only don't I hear them, but I'm not even there.

But what if I can't find a rooming house? How could I live outdoors in my condition, so poor that I don't have two pennies to rub together, as unfit to confront the dangers of the world as a newly-born chick whose feet have been tied and beak filed down before being abandoned in a deep jungle just when the big cats awaken with a roar, perform a moulinet on their back legs tipped with powerful claws, and prepare to eat everything that can be eaten around them in order to satiate themselves until their next nap?

Another question might cross my mind: how was Sixtus paying for his hotel? Well, he wasn't. He no longer paid for it, if, that is, he ever had. That one, the violinist, the owner, the Daisy Pushers, the VIRUM, the SNOT, he tolerated his presence in the deserted establishment not through generosity (a nice hypothesis that makes you fall over laughing), but because he'd become attached to his whipping boy! Moreover, money gave the owner the ideal pretext to nettle Sixtus at any time with facetious questions like, "Tell me Sixtus, you're paying me today, right? I'm not mistaken? That's what we decided?" Or even more bitterly malicious: "By the way, Sixtus, thanks. I got your envelope. No? Well then, whose was it? You're the only one here! My word, I must have dreamed it!"

The worst was when my hunger drove me to the kitchen despite everything. I was sure to find Luc there, near the cupboard, his mouth filled with humiliating comments concerning the fact that he fed me for free, that I'd have the shirt off his back next, that I was pulling the wool over his eyes, that I was really the wolf and he the lamb—or purely malicious comments, with no bearing on the situation, surfacing like a hair in your soup, or rather, like a wig suddenly flung into the bottom of a soup pot, for example about my physical appearance—he who was as ugly as sin—more precisely about my hair, which according to him was falling out by the fistful (untrue! it was long, greasy, white with dust, and full of knots, but I always had more than he did—could he deny it? Well, yes he could! He would respond, pouting with extreme skepticism, which made him even more hideous than before: hmmmmm, we'd have to count them—he whose scalp you could see in several places, if, that is, you could call that palpitating membrane, spotted and sticky with sweat, a scalp), about my nose, which was too large, about my ears, about the way I walked, about everything, about every aspect of my body, about my entire being! My nose! What about his? His nose, that swollen blister, which became stuffed up at the slightest infection? (CEO of SNOT! Hadn't he retained one single sample of his nasal deturgescent?) His eyes, those bulging abscesses that stared sadly at one another? His ears, those crumpled curtains, in which every word I said to him was smothered and lost? His mouth, that restless wound where his own words so frequently became lost, turned back down into his chest and descended all the way to his bowels, where they spoke only to him? And I'm not even going to discuss his walk: slow, labored, chaotic, disjointed, forced as he was by I-don't-know-what skeletal disease to perform a million contortions and as many pained expressions just to put one foot in front of the other!

His usual threat concerned the following morning's coffee. Problem with the supplier. Careless supplier. "Or maybe it was my own carelessness? I don't recall. In any case, Sixtus, the result's the same. Tomorrow morning you'll either have to wander through the streets, braced against the arctic blasts of early spring, or content yourself with stagnant, tepid tap water. Your choice."

He was lying: I never needed to leave the hotel. And then I'd accuse him of lying (especially since he would slip other fabrications into our conversation: he claimed to have been married previously and to be the father of many children!), we would raise our voices, and it wasn't uncommon that we'd come to blows: "Take that! Smack! Pow! Bing Bang Boom! This'll shut you up, you bore! Ooof! I'll black both your goddamn eyes! No, it's not nighty-night time yet! No, not at all, in fact, it's time for your ears to get a little attention! That's right, I'll pull them back and tie them in a big knot behind your head! Come on! Here you go! And another and another! Sure, maybe I'll stuff those flaps right up your nose! Very nice. Oh, your mouth is moving! Can you still talk? Nope. I didn't think so. That cement you're covered in hardens very quickly. Turn around please . . . there . . . there . . . there! And now, when you've managed to get your sorry, starved self off the ground, let me know. I'm counting on you!"

More bark than bite, it's true: three bumps and three scratches that six dabs with a wet cloth took care of—with the exception, however, of an injury to my lower abdomen that he accidentally inflicted once with his claws, and from which I have a scar to this day (to this very day!).

DOCTORS AND PHILOSOPHERS

How did all this childishness end up? Well, I would usually return to my slovenly hole on the third floor and stuff my face with everything I'd been able to swipe from the kitchen. Nothing very filling, nor very fresh, nor very nourishing, alas! If it's true, as doctors and philosophers have asserted, that the seat of the soul is the stomach, then the caustic slop with which I would occasionally fertilize my gastric garden at the Rats and Vermin Hotel could never have given me the energy necessary to escape and put my plan into action: specifically, my intention to live out an unprecedented adventure, to meet the adorable Queene, etc. Oh, no. Even less so since I couldn't even swallow the stuff. I couldn't get it down. Couldn't even chew it. Or, rather, it was so difficult to get down that just the movement of my jaw would make the food come out of my mouth again, either all at once, or in chunks of confetti-like pieces, instead of pushing them back down to where the natural slope of the throat was beckoning to them.

THE WORST THUNDERSTORMS

The sleep that would follow these repasts didn't merit the name sleep. It was a kind of prolonged electrocution via a thousand different kinds of internal nervous discharges, a protracted and devilish dance that I preferred to break off as quickly as possible—sometimes employing subterfuge: I would feign the sleep of the just, lying on my back, eyelids closed and my fists clenched on either side of my face. Thus I would force myself to remain immobile and would imitate the loud breathing of someone deep in an animal-like sleep, my gaping mouth sucking in the room's thick, fetid air, before emitting snores that rumbled louder than the worst summer thunderstorm echoing off the crags of the most tightly grouped circle of mountains. But this act deflated me just as much as, how should I put it, just as much as it would have elated me if it hadn't only been an act, yes, the equilibrium was perfect—until a terribly violent protest on the part of every fiber of my being united in a joint attack would propel me out of bed like some scalded dog, and I'd find myself coiled like a snake in the bathroom sink, where the tap provided only stagnant and tepid water, as the owner quite rightly said, if in fact that thin-haired, disjointed gnome really was the owner, and not a simple manager. Maybe he was nothing but a pitiful manager with delusions of grandeur, always bowing down to the owner!

Married! War photographer! Father of many children!

ANIMAL CRIES

In my opinion, it was the cold that prevented me from sleeping. The cold as much as the noise of the boiler, on the rare occasions it would ignite, a noise that I, more tightly strung than an archer's bow, would fretfully await every hour of every day, despite the fact that it only started up once in a blue moon, since some-one had set it on low. It could have been turned up so we'd be warmer, but (without even mentioning the manager's cupidity or tightfistedness), when it was turned up, millions of sparks would fly out of its tiny holes whenever the boiler ignited, making it incandescent, though without necessarily heating the radiators in the hotel. Okay, so you turn it all the way up. You head back to your room. You wait and wait, but you're still chilled to the bone. You touch the radiators: cold. Not to mention it was a fire hazard. On the other hand, when it was on low—that is, when it was, theoretically, working—it would switch on only once in a blue moon. And during these long intervals, it seemed to build up a stronger and stronger desire to ignite, a rage thwarted by its low setting. So that when it finally did ignite, the noise of the explosion was such that I would let out different animal cries—which, as my mind was in such disarray, I would always jumble together. I would confusedly imitate the staccato howl of a hare, the doleful warbling of a boar, or the stubborn barking of a fly. I must have gone through every single cry of every single animal in creation, in my opinion.

The first day I was there, the owner (who that day, the very first day, evinced a hypocritical politeness) placed a small elec-tric heater at my disposal, but it only barely warmed your an-kles, and its heat arrived with the roar of a fighter squadron taking off for a decisive attack, the wait for which had frayed everyone's nerves.

I must tell you that noises terrify me.

Admittedly, an almost absolute silence pervaded the hotel. Deserted hotel, dead planet. But, but, there was the boiler, and the space heater, and a million other noises that my imagination, agitated by the lunatic whims of my own frayed nerves, would attribute to the most terrifying origins (with great effort, a motorcyclist had carried his bike into his apartment and was revving it up, or else an army of roofers had invaded the area and were replacing metal roof tiles one by one)—not to mention the insignificant, yet frequent, even continuous noise of the thousands of insects that would smash themselves into the bare lightbulb hanging in my room. It really didn't take more than that for my heart to jump with such force that fireworks in the sky would have seemed less precipitous than an old man raising his eyelids and for me to end up letting out one of those famous cries, the growl of a killer whale perhaps, the cheeping of a bear or the braying of a rat, which would wake up the owner (let's just call him the owner, once and for all), curious as a cat, but evil as a scorpion, so evil that he would use the opportunity to bombard me with his irrelevant and gratuitously vengeful questions—By the way, Sixtus, how old are you? Oh, really? I thought you were older, or younger (though my answer never varied), or else: Did you dye your hair? No? I thought you were dark-haired (or blond), etc. though everything was always the same—until, occasionally, we would finally come to blows.

Frequently, at the slightest tick! the slightest ssss! or the slightest blurp! I would press my ear against the wall, the floor, the ceiling in an effort to pinpoint its source. Why? Because I was afraid that

that tick, ssss, or blurp were not out there, but in here, in my ears, in my head: I try to get away from this planet, bearing two pillows, I scale the highest mountain of the farthest planet, and there I press the pillows over my ears, but I still hear tick, ssss, or blurp!

To escape, escape from the hotel!

THOUGHTS, THOUGHT

I was thinking of something . . . but it has just escaped me. But that brings me to something else that I wanted to talk about, which is that, at the hotel, I'd recently had more and more difficulty thinking, precisely because my thoughts all escaped me. I'd hurl myself on them, whomp! but they'd slip away and then smash themselves painfully against the walls of my cranial gaol, clink. Then they would return to wherever they'd started from, I would hurl myself on them again, and so on and so forth, clink. Or sometimes I'd act as if I were ignoring them. A miscalculation: that would only agitate them further, leading to even greater pain, and my poor head would feel like it was about to explode, like a pressure cooker with no safety valve, thrown into the mouth of an erupting volcano—but there were worse things.

Worse? Worse. At certain times I had neither the strength to pursue them nor to feign indifference, and yet I detected no agitation on their part, no movement—but I could hear a sort of suspicious interior silence, as if a thief were leaving your house with everything you own—as if someone were filching my thoughts—or as if my thoughts themselves were flowing out of me, obviously not like a spring, cheerfully bubbling out of a moss-covered cave and fertilizing the florid countryside during the summer, but more akin to the frigid, moribund water that leaks from a forgotten reservoir, cold and riddled with rusty holes in the deepest recesses of a vanished land.

ROCKABYE BABY

One evening, shortly before my departure (just hours before my departure, truth be told: I only set aside my quill to make my escape), I resolved to put the story of my sojourn at the Rats and Vermin Hotel down in writing. Alas, I didn't succeed. I learned that I wasn't master of my own hand. It was stronger than I, yes stronger than I. I started to trace various letters, which were disproportionately stretched out, at times vertically—then they seemed like they'd been frightened by some ghastly spectacle, ready to escape, to dart off towards the top of the page with the speed of a hummingbird or towards the bottom as swiftly as a sword through water—at times horizontally—and then they seemed, though still just as terrified, as if they wanted to flatten themselves, hollow themselves out, to merge with the bottom of the page—or else, at other times, not just inconsonant vertically or horizontally, but in every direction, extended, bloated, as if stricken with some illness, which, not satisfied with swelling them from the inside, tormented their most miniscule imperfections unrelentingly in order to turn them all into nasty excrescences—or even, yes, these letters diminished, desiccated, derogated to the point of invisibility, fashioning a kind of dotted line. These lines would hesitate, tarry, dawdle, prevaricate, turning back and sprawling out in lascivious meanderings, or, on the contrary, they would tumble down to the very bottom of the page, which would inevitably stop them—but enough! I said to myself, throwing pen and paper over my shoulder. Enough!

Anyone who might care to recite the tale of this battle aloud should scream that "enough," scream it so that they can understand my impotent rage. And yet, even if they really gave the performances everything they had—blood, sweat, and tears—they still couldn't scream loudly enough. On paper, I'm forced to write "enough" in the same way I would jot down nice things like "rockabye baby"—whereas yelling, well, I would need to stab the page with a dagger, a dagger glistening with the blood of a bull I myself had slaughtered.

But enough. We absolutely need to calm down before leaving the hotel, otherwise we'll never make it. Let's content ourselves by noting that the vicissitudes of existence had led me to stay in a 12th class hotel in the city's twelfth arrondissement. (Here and there, in a lounge, down a hallway, a painting, torn and coated with grime, or a sculpture, egregiously chipped, even crumbling down to its pedestal, would nevertheless recall an undoubtedly more glorious age.) A hotel run by a malicious and miserly owner, or manager: Luc, Luc M., you know, the man who claimed to have had a wife and children in the olden days, and who whenever possible would plunge a scathing knife of cruelty in my back just as my feet tickled the precipice of the bottomless pit of despair—but enough, enough on the chapter in the hotel, for pity's sake, not another word, I beseech myself, if I utter another word I'll make the sign of the cross with one hand and sentence myself to hard labor with the other!

I threw my pen and paper behind me.

A little voice, initially a soft murmur, was wailing in my ears now. The state of conclusion I had reached at The Rats was so extreme that death outside the hotel was preferable to staying put. "Run away, run away!" the voice told me incessantly, growing louder each second.

A WORD FROM ME, AND . . .

The owner, with his face—already less than pleasing—bathed in virescent tears (a simple aggravation of his normal, chronically infectious state, or the expression of his parting sorrow, as he alleged?), came to tell me that he had taken his violin out of his armoire, cleaned it, changed the strings . . . A word from me and he would go get it. And he would play me a little tune before my departure, an old divertimento of his own composition.

Play the violin for me! He, who hadn't played for an eternity, if he had ever played at all (but I believe that he had), if he had ever even owned a violin! Moreover, knotted and deformed as his body was, could he even hold the instrument correctly? What about drawing the bow? No, not possible. So? An ultimate provocation on his part, an ultimate act of malevolence so that I would leave with my body and soul filled with this malevolence, which would taint an already arduous journey? Or else was he really hoping to keep me there? To hurt me? Waiting for me to tell him: "Well okay, Luc, fetch thy fife and play a little something that'll make me stay?" I don't know now and never will, because, hands covering my ears, I acted deaf: he could just head back to his squalid room, slip between his dirty sheets, and make all the noise he wanted, all by himself, that's what my livid silence told him—and Luc obeyed me like a child.

He turned around, shaken by another spasm, a spasm of tears. But even today (today!) I don't feel guilty about my reaction: if it were true that when he played he played with such exhausting and dangerous fervor, then he might have died right in front of my eyes. I had just saved his life.

III

THE JOURNEY

FROM A TO Z

I left in the morning. Walking aimlessly at first, I soon found myself on a long, straight street, which I followed because it was straight. This street changed in name and appearance (wide or narrow, architecture from one period or another, tree-lined or not, deserted or busy, street musicians or not, etc.) but it kept going straight for, maybe, well I don't know, a couple dozen kilometers so that I ended up crossing the city from A to Z, then a large, dark wood, also from A to Z, and then a ritzy suburb. But then I stopped, phew! at L. when I caught a glimpse of—believe it or not—the building from my dreams: old, solid and firmly planted on the Earth's surface in the heart of a large garden. It was a holiday, and many of the shutters were closed. No light on the fourth, fifth, or sixth floors. Everything was going according to plan. I would move into the fifth floor, well protected by the fourth and sixth, and then I answer to no one.

But let's wait. I would be putting the cart before the horse if I didn't mention the superhuman efforts I undertook to cross the city. I was hungry, tired, and afraid. I had a headache (a constant pounding in my head). Every few feet I would move my crumpled canvas suitcase from one hand to the other, not because it was so laden with my worldly possessions, the hypothesis is so amusing you might fall over and die laughing (all told, I was probably only dragging five or six bits of junk), but rather because the hand holding the suitcase was so cold. So, I would switch from one hand to the other, thrusting the other one, the freezing one, into the pocket of my raincoat, which was too light, and where it hardly warmed up at all, for the spring was cold and gloomy. It had been gloomy all morning, to the point that daybreak seemed like nightfall.

All manner of destitution: with the drive of a snail on whose back some prankster places a heavier and heavier load, it took an unprecedented level of courage for me to traverse the many kilometers between the cursed hotel and that fateful building.

If only I can cross the threshold!

Indeed, I dread these buildings in which the rich ensconce themselves. First intercom: "Yes?" Sixtus: "I'm here to see X." "One moment, please." After having run the gauntlet through two other intercoms, been scrutinized on four screens, and stripped by five searches, X's bodyguard cracks open the first of the twelve doors.

However, it was easy: I came in with someone else, a woman, who didn't even notice me. She lived on the first floor and immediately headed off, without seeing me, almost as if she was doing it on purpose, almost as if we had previously colluded to pretend not knowing one another.

I was inside and no longer outside. But my suffering along the way was so excruciating, searching my soul with every step as it were, that I hadn't really seen my surroundings and might have believed that I had simply passed through a doorway that led from that cursed hotel to this fateful building.

I proffered a silent thank you to the woman. Without her, what could I have done except scale the building's facade from balcony to balcony up to the fifth floor, where I would shatter an *œil-de-bœuf*, with all the difficulties that you can very well imagine, given the state I was in, and considering the fact that I had never distinguished myself with my climbing abilities. Anyone who wished to sing my praises truthfully would not say that I was an ace climber. But with great effort, the suitcase handle between my teeth, I first heave myself up on the patio railing of the first apartment where I squat for a few seconds like a distraught toad, my hands between my feet, then I stand up, grasp the concrete floor of the second floor balcony and pull myself up by my arms, inch by inch—a concomitant balancing of my body, right and left—then hup! an agonizing thrust, and hup! one foot on the edge of the floor, then, initially using only the strength of my wrists, and quickly, very quickly with the help of my feet, I scale the rail of the second floor balcony upon which once again I find myself precariously balanced, squatting, hands between my feet, as winded as some old hag, and so on and so forth until I reach the fifth floor.

Which leaves the *œil-de-bœuf*. My hand inside a flowerpot, from which I have previously removed the flowers, I break its thick glass. Thunk! Craassshhh! Then I crawl through the opening, terrified by the idea of remaining forever with my shoulders caught.

But that's not it at all. I easily enter the building thanks to a person who hardly even notices me.

QUAM JUVAT . . .

The tenants' names were posted on a rather large sign. I managed to read them. Fifth floor: Louis and Armelle M. Admittedly, my lips sounded out the words one by one, as if I were just learning to read. But the memory of letters, who had run off while I was living in the hotel, losing all their flesh as a result, skeletons seeking refuge in the most inaccessible depths of my being, was now returning. The letters became plumper and more active with each passing moment, preening themselves and arrogantly crowing on center stage.

Victory!

Of course, I still had to force open the fifth floor door. But once this obstacle was overcome, I could luxuriate in an ideal environment: delectable food, properly calibrated furnace, snug, clean bed—what pleasure after the journey's hardships and the weather's severity! As the ancient poet wrote: *quam juvat immites ventos audire cubantem et dominam tenero continuisse sinu aut, gelidas vernalis aquas cum fuderit Auster, securum somnos igne juvante sequi!*

I headed towards the elevator.

IV

OUTLAW

WRONG NUMBER

Fifth floor.

I thought I heard Luc: "Now what?" What do you mean, now what, Luc? "Yes, Sixtus, how are you going to get inside?" How am I going to get inside? Well, I'll turn the oversized doorknob and the door will open!

I turned the doorknob, and the door opened. Overcoming my astonishment—for, in spite of my impertinent response, I swear I was astonished—I entered and immediately closed the door.

I turned on the lights.

I followed a long hallway decorated with paintings.

Another surprise was waiting for me: in a large living room, two fifty-year-old men (one of whom had a ruddy, shrunken head, a glow worm's head, and the other gray hair so long that I thought it was a woman at first) were lying on the floor, bathed in their own blood. Each held a gun. On the table, a small satchel filled with banknotes. I also saw a keychain with thousands of keys, the type of keychain that outlaws use to open any door. What had happened? Well, one of the two men had broken in to steal the money. Or to take back the money he believed to be his. The other (Louis M.) had surprised him, and they'd killed one another. That's what had happened.

I grabbed the satchel in a most nonchalant manner and decided to move to the fourth or sixth floor, too bad, somewhere other than the Ms' flat.

I left.

Another surprise on the landing: I was on the sixth floor! My numb, shaking, anxious finger, secretly influenced, moreover, by a number whose name was somewhat like my own, Sixtus, had pressed six and not five!

Very well then. I went to get the keychain and calmly descended one floor.

Of those thousands of keys, the one hundred and fifty-second opened the Ms' door.

INCOGNITO

Two letters had been slipped under the door.

The boiler. I pressed some buttons so that it immediately emitted the pleasant murmur of a million insects.

Armelle M. was a very beautiful brunette, with an even face and an intense look, as the dozens of photographs throughout the apartment attested. Taken by Louis M., who worshipped her? No doubt.

I counted the bills. Two million francs! I was two million francs the richer!

What to do? First off, eat, drink, soothe my headache, bathe, and put on some clean clothes (pilfered from Louis). And then? Leave the apartment? That would be a shame. It was nice here at the Ms'. Stay? They can start any number of investigations, pound at my door, I won't open for them, won't hear them, won't be home? Unless the Ms are not on vacation and will return tonight after an enjoyable evening with friends? Thirst, with its thousands of sharp, forked, abrasive tongues consumed my throat: I put future considerations aside and held to my decision to regain my strength before anything else.

I had never seen a refrigerator as well stocked with victuals as the Ms'. A fierce, unending war could break out, and they wouldn't be left wanting. I settled in next to a radiator and drank and drank. The radiator was burning hot. Burn-ing! You couldn't touch it. My feet, yes. They were only vaguely warm. Fro-zen! The radiator turned stone cold in a couple of seconds. I sapped the warmth of several radiators like this, but they quickly became burning hot again.

The medicine cabinet in the bathroom contained enough drugs to cure most of the world's diseases. Soon, phew, it was as if the kindest nurse in the world was layering more and more cotton gauze between the pounding hammers and my skull.

I showered (holy terror of bathrooms, too much water), washed my hair and body, which suddenly took on the appearance of a human being once more, brushed my teeth, which I hadn't brushed since earliest antiquity, and dressed from head to foot. (Louis M. must have had the same build as I had, for I slipped into his clothes as easily as if they were mine, even though, new or nearly so, the clothing was his.)

Then yum yum munch crunch chomp chomp, I ate like no one ever has. A satisfied warmth overcame me. I was even too warm. I even ended up turning down the heating.

FRRT

I explored the apartment in more detail. I'll pass over its magnificence, the vastness of its rooms, the furnishings, the chandeliers and wall hangings from Spanish palaces, the works of art. From what I deduced, Louis M. was the CEO of a financial corporation, FRRT, whose role was to reduce the loss of capital to foreign countries. Armelle M. was a speech therapist who worked with both those who could no longer speak, and those who had never been able to.

What a beauty! When you looked at the photo hanging just to the right as you entered the living room, for example, you couldn't believe that such beauty existed. You walked around the room hitting your head in disbelief.

The thermometer had fallen to 95 degrees.

AN UNSEALED LETTER

So, the letters that had been slipped under the door weren't stamped. I picked them up. The first one (the furthest from the door, very far away in fact—too far, methinks: might it not have been set there? Yes, that was exactly it!), the first one had but one word on the envelope, "Armelle," and the envelope wasn't sealed.

It read:

Dearest Armelle,

I will not be home tonight. I am going far away and will not return. A difficult, but foreseeable decision, as you well know, my dear. How heartbreaking! More for me than for you? I believe so. I don't think you're mean or evil—no, but life can't go on like this.

I'll tell you again that the physical difficulties have nothing to do with it.

I am moving to another city, perhaps abroad. To start over . . . My God! Is it better to write these words than to be without hands, to read them than to be blind or illiterate, my forever beloved?

Someday, I will call. As for right now, I couldn't endure any contact between us. I would shatter like an incredibly fragile piece of porcelain hit by an incredibly destructive projectile.

I'm leaving you the Sublima (the keys are on my desk). I'm leaving you everything; I'm taking nothing. If you do go to Spain, please be careful.

I love you with all my soul,

Louis.

So at least the husband wouldn't be bothering me today. As for Armelle . . . But let's wait.

But not for long, because the other letter, addressed simply to "Mr. Louis M." said:

> Dear Mr. Louis M.,
>
> This afternoon I kidnapped your wife, Armelle. Oh yes, you can pick your jaw up off the floor and stick your eyeballs back in their sockets, I kidnapped her all right. I'm sure you'll be quite keen to see her alive again, by giving me what must be an insignificant sum for someone such as you, the CEO of FRRT: one million francs. Just seconds before 8:00 P.M., have your hand on the telephone. It will ring at exactly 8:00 P.M.
>
>   Talk to you soon.

No signature.

At 8:00 P.M. the phone rang.

I picked up.

"Mister Louis M.?" "Yes."

V

THE EXCHANGE

SUBLIMA

Dressed like royalty, I appeared at the exit of the apartment's underground parking garage behind the wheel of a Sublima that was painted master-of-the-universe red. The car seemed at one with me, such was my driving prowess, the best in the world (memories flooded back, coming from I don't know where, nearly erasing images of the hotel and its owner's vile abuse—who would that poor devil turn his murderous rage against now? My God, so much blood in that sixth-floor apartment! A carnage in no way comparable to the three scratches between the manager of the Rats and me, yet let's not forget my nasty little ventral scar), yes, the best in the world: always the first off the line, already shifting into fourth while the green luminescence of the traffic light hadn't yet registered with certainty on the retinas of the other drivers, hardly even slowing down in the middle of the most congested traffic jams. How's that? Well, by all means possible: I drive on the left as much as on the right, on the sidewalks as much as on the road, in reverse, on two wheels, either on one side, on the front wheels, reminiscent of a frenzied, sniffing dog, or on the rears like a bucking bull—or even on the roof. One day, tearing down the M.s' street the wrong way, I end up in front of the N.-D. de L. church doing a hundred and sixty kilometers an hour, I've got to do something quick, a violent turn of the wheel during which my twisted arms look like a pretzel, the car rolls over three times and keeps going on, the roof scraping against the pavement and spitting sparks until rue de Château, where the car stops at a red light, you know, right next to the famous designer store, M. A police officer arrives. Well, he says to me. Well nothing, I'm waiting for the light, I say. The light changes. I jam the car into first with great gusto, and so intimate is the bond that I have always had with my vehicles that the car continues on its roof down rue de Château, shaking, and again spitting out a spray of sparks on the asphalt, the officer wildly gesticulating: hey, hey! ho, ho! whoa, whoa, whoa!

QUEENE

Rue du Régiment.

The dead end off Régiment. The café, a few yards down the dead-end street. I recognize Armelle M. and her magnificent black hair, Armelle seated in the exact spot the man on the phone had indicated—but I mustn't stop or approach her—later, after delivering the ransom—or else a bullet from I don't know where will kill me. Suddenly, I'm afraid. Afraid of the sniper who is surely monitoring me. Where is he hiding? On a rooftop, onto which he would have climbed with the stomach-turning speed of an ape? In a doorway, crouched against the floor, frozen with the implacable immobility of a crocodile? Unless he is waiting for me at our rendezvous point, ready to attack me and steal the money, and I'll never see Armelle again?

Courage, Sixtus! I continue driving according to the instructions: first street on the right, then the second right after that.

At number 9 I stop in front of a small townhouse.

I place the satchel, which now contains one million francs, in the miniscule, deserted doorman's office, and I take off.

Then what should have happened doesn't.

Let me explain.

I sit down in front of the woman who was waiting at the Dragon Café. Yes, she was very beautiful, her beauty was one of a kind, and yes, she looked like Armelle M.—but this person with light eyes and hair that was too smooth and shiny was not Armelle M.!

I questioned her. She answered all the more honestly because she didn't know what was going on. Queene (that was her name) had always earned her living illegally. Earlier this morning an unknown man had called and offered her a large sum of money simply for being in a certain café at a certain time with such-and-such a wig. A man (me) would then arrive, would be disappointed, cross, furious, would ask questions to which she would be unable to respond, and that would be it. I would end up leaving, and she would have made a handsome sum for little effort.

But I didn't leave. After she had removed her wig, with the movements and expression of a child who had been caught, and freed her naturally blonde hair, I had no desire to leave her.

If Armelle was the most beautiful of all women, Queene was a goddess briefly blessing Earth with her presence.

I told her my story, and we attempted to reconstruct that of the others: the kidnapper, did he plan on demanding a second ransom, maybe even a third? Or maybe (this was Queene's idea) the speech therapist was an accomplice and had decided—Louis's kind-hearted assessment of his wife's lack of wickedness would then have been erroneous—to harass her husband, to ruin him, to destroy him? We would never know. And, as the minutes passed by, we forgot, for the immediate bond that had united Queene and me occupied our minds completely.

VI

THE SECRET

THE YEAR 5555

We left the café. The streets were teeming with people. Friday night, in this neighborhood, you can imagine. Friday the fifth. Friday, the fifth day of the week. Of the month of May, the fifth month of the year? Of the year 5555? Of course not. I'm not talking about a hypothetical evening of an invented year, but of a real evening at the beginning of spring. It was a bit chilly, and we were walking through the busy downtown streets and Queene—a very young woman, younger than I had originally thought (because of the black wig, no doubt)—Queene told me that she herself had been living in a small, furnished hotel room in the northern suburbs for quite some time, and that, moreover, she had been born in that area, in a most destitute neighborhood—that, later in life, dubious company . . . I listened to her—I listened to every word her adorable mouth uttered—but all that mattered to me was the miracle of her presence: she was beautiful, gentle, as pure as an angel—and she could have laid claim, in spite of her indigent origins, to the title of queen of the world—and she was at my side!

I found what I was looking for in an evening paper: a house abroad for rent for one month (in M., in Spain, the city where I was born).

The business was settled in two telephone calls. Soon, in a car I'd rented in Queene's name simply to please her, an almost new, red Sublima that was even more magnificent than the Ms', we crossed the congested, one might even say paralyzed city, but what did I care? That red dot, whose movements couldn't really be followed due to the composition of human neck muscles and the limited mobility of the eye in its orbit, that was me—and, on the highway all the way to M., Madrid, I treated the accelerator like a scorpion set to sting me—such was my persistence in crushing it despite its stridulation, with such parsimony did I give it any space to move.

THE VULTURE

Queene was sleeping, turned towards me, her right hand resting on my right shoulder. Occasionally I'd watch her sleeping, and an unfamiliar feeling of joy would sweep over me.

Dawn broke. We crossed the Spanish border.

Nearing M., I heard what sounded like the screeching of a vulture overhead. I raised my eyes. I spied an enormous bird. I believe it was a vulture, that it had seen me, and that it was tracing the incertitude of my life in the sky.

The shops were opening. We filled the Sublima with provisions, clothes, and everything necessary for a very long stay.

La Casa Margarita (located not too far from the famous workshop of the luthier Miguel M. Hermanos, formerly Auelio Esteso), had twenty-four windows, eight of which overlooked a tropical garden.

We explored the house—as spacious as a hotel, and whose magnificence I will pass over (the number and vastness of its rooms, the furnishings, the wall hangings, the chandeliers, the works of art), and the garden, so immense that it didn't seem like we were in the heart of my hometown, but out in nature—with the joy of children on the first day of summer vacation.

Queene went to take a shower.

A THOUSAND QUESTIONS

It was then, while continuing to rummage about in *La Casa Margarita*, that I discovered, in a book-filled, second-floor office overlooking the street, the infamous manuscript, at the back of the bottom drawer of a dark, bulky Andalusian chest of drawers—an anonymous manuscript written in a neat, clear, regular hand, addressed to no specific person and without title or signature. I formulated a thousand hypotheses: a manuscript composed by the owner? Or by one of his descendents or ancestors? Or by a houseguest? Or a stranger who may have broken into the house and who, in lieu of pilfering the drawer's contents may have on the contrary smuggled something in . . . ?

I don't know. What's important is that I immediately decided to conceal the manuscript from Queene, for fear that she be driven to despair, for fear that she deem our fate hopelessly sealed, for fear that she believe I had never left the Rats, or that we would forever remain prisoners of *La Casa Margarita*, or that we had already met an infinite number of times but had forgotten these encounters, as well as a thousand other terrifying mysteries.

I surreptitiously reread the manuscript in fragments, and at the end of that first Madridian day, I reached a point of profound understanding of the tale (bravo, Sixtus!), all the way to the very end.

Yes, a terrifying mystery! A thousand questions tormented me, a thousand answers haunted me: that life could not last all of life, that the unearthed manuscript was nothing other than the world without Queene and me, as well as thousands of others—and I held my beloved tightly in my arms, as if someone were trying to spirit her away—but however fervently others may have contemplated abducting her, an entire army besieging *La Casa Margarita* wouldn't have risked it, with a glance the commanding general would have understood that it wasn't prudent, that they should furtively retreat, without a sound, without the click of boots, such is the order he would have intimated to his men in a voice so weak his soldiers would have strained their eyes trying to decipher the words on his lips.

SCAR

Night fell. We undressed in the loveliest of the bedrooms, all of which were the loveliest, or perhaps it was Queene's own loveliness that transformed everything—rooms, cities, the world.

I was ashamed of the small scar on my lower abdomen, or rather I would have been ashamed to tell Queene about Luc M. and our skirmishes. Although she didn't question me about it,

I really had to say something. The need to lie made me mutter, nearly inaudibly, a number of long-winded explanations: that, being chased down by two Spanish fighting bulls, I had crawled over some barbed wire, that I had fallen on a knife, an inadvertently stuck-up blade in the ground, that I had swallowed a rabbit bone, which one day broke through my skin when I was bending over to pick up a coin, that I had had it from birth, that I was born like this, with this small slit near my sex, that I had almost been a woman—then I lay down next to her in the four-poster baldachin-style standing bed, which had been offered by Henri IV's mistress to the King of Spain in 1590, a bed whose two decorated ceilour panels, in light gray and gold, were divided into three sections bordered by an elaborate wooden frame sculpted with flowers (tulips) and supported by four columns turned with incredibly skillful extravagance; in a word it was a museum-worthy piece, whose square, draped silhouette rose in the middle of the room, the fabric simply capped on the corners by four finials with plumes when the curtains were lowered, whereas when they were raised (as was the case tonight), you couldn't make out either the bed itself, as it was hidden by the tester, or the columns, hidden by the cantoons and bonegraces, or the canopy itself, hidden by the valances.

And it was in this bed, a true masterpiece, a kind of room within a room, that Queene and I . . .

SEXUAL ENCOUNTER, 1

Oh! An infinite desire overtook me, and the throbbing of my flesh induced by just the look in her bright eyes was enough to unleash liquid eruptions, torrential in their restless brutality and fluvial in the enormity of their output, whose endless amatory inundation flooded my beloved's body.

But alas, Queene, as I already knew . . .

Yet she wanted to, in spite of . . . for she had never experienced sexual pleasure—nevertheless she wished with all her soul that I remain inside her—and my desire, as if made eternal by this wish, spread in a new deluge worthy of the dawn of the Earth, and so it was until the end of our stay at *La Casa Margarita*.

The following day came, then another, and still more. Our month's vacation slipped by.

One night, I thought I made out Luc M. claudicating across the hallway, the violinist, the pharmacist, the photographer, the man who had kept memory alive. But no, it was a vision, a shadow, a phantom, the phantom of Luc perhaps, ruminating on his own sorrow at not having been able to play the violin for my departure.

Eating delicious food, sleeping as if we were in the heart of silence itself, uniting—under the previously mentioned conditions, alas—we rarely left the room and almost never left the house, but then again yes, we did at least once, the night of the concert.

VII

BETWEEN FABRIC AND FLESH

THE CONCERT, 1

There was a large crowd on the famed plaza Santa Margarita. Queene and I weren't very comfortable; we had found only one seat for the two of us.

We were waiting for the conductor to appear. Occasionally I would kiss Queene. Pulling my head back, I could see her lips glistening with my own essence. I would then reach out and lightly caress her breast through the fabric of her dress. (During this season it was warm in M., and we were lightly dressed.) Queene wouldn't reciprocate by touching my chest, but she'd take my hand and slip it herself against her breast, between fabric and flesh, there, where her heart was beating, and the charm of her features, which during moments such as this would have made the blood of an antique statue rush, transfixed me.

I was afraid. (Secretly, by joining the crowd gathered for the concert, we were attempting to unite more completely. But what would be the result?) My fears increased when, with an overly forceful upstroke of his baton, the conductor gouged out a piece of his eye as he signaled the opening chord to the orchestra, even though some of the musicians hadn't even taken their instruments out of their cases, or still had their backs to him, dusting off their chairs, or were absorbed in a vicious argument with their neighbor behind them, frequently coming to blows, or were reading the newspaper, or manifesting their desire not to play in a thousand other ways—the pianist was wiping his glasses on his sleeve, the flutist was tying a gag around her mouth, the cellist, who had rinsed his clothes in a basin, was now wringing them out, the clarinetist was firing shots in the air, the saxophonist was lying down on the ground to take a nap, the horn player was devouring a roasted rabbit thigh, the contrabassist was gargling with a liquid so bitter it made him grimace, which he then spit into the f-hole of his double-bass, the trumpeter looked saddened by the frail and melancholic sounds his intestinal gasses were producing through his trumpet whose mouthpiece he had painfully shoved up his backside, seven violinists were blowing into their violins, the eighth was taking a photograph of the conductor, two percussionists were playing dice on a drum while accusing each other of cheating, the harpist was performing one somersault after another—so that, at the precise moment when the lush opening chords of Miguel Padilla's (1899–1956) symphony should have burst forth, as noted in the program, announcing with an apocalyptic cacophony the work's myriad

themes, one could only hear the hoarse crackling of a flageo-
let belonging to the only orchestra member who had followed
the violent indications of the conductor (who had split his lip
open on his bony knees, having contorted his entire being in a
fit of rage), a crackling cut short by the intimidated musician
who hid his beet-red face behind his music held crumpled in
his hands.

THE CONCERT, 2

My fears grew again when the musicians finally deigned to en-
gage in activities that more closely evoked the idea of music
(with the exception of the cellist, for nothing could convince
him to pick up his bow, neither prayers, nor threats, nor blows,
which he adroitly avoided while simultaneously hanging his
clothes on the strings of his cello so that they could dry in the
evening breeze). Indeed, it seemed wildly obvious that playing
together with precision and humility, or even diligently playing
their own parts, or at least using their instruments in a manner that wasn't contrary to the natural order of the world was
the last thing on their minds: the pianist was striking the keys
of the piano with his teeth in a burst of ostensible hilarity that
showed no true joy, the harpist, exhausted from her pirouettes,
was snoring, eyes closed, chin resting on the harp, the percussionists were hitting the drums with their reproductive organs, flailing them about, producing muffled sounds that were
drowned out by cries of agony, the flutist was producing such
strange sounds that Queene initially thought some change had

fallen out of her pocket and onto the ground, the trumpeter was now pretending to blow into his instrument while he was actually squeezing a vulgar-looking rubber bulb behind his back, the contrabassist was shaking his bass to make the various little creatures he had previously plunged into his bitter gargle croak, the clarinetist was blowing whole-heartedly into his clarinet, he went completely red and his head doubled in size, but this was because his instrument was plugged up, and when he finally unplugged it, an appalling bellow ensued, making people's hair stand on end and all the nearby dogs scamper away—and yet, and yet . . .

COINCIDENCES

Yet, there was no lack of felicitous encounters between the sounds, which occasionally seemed orchestrated to be played together: this is how I shall always remember the miracle of the final *tutti*. All the musicians, undoubtedly eager not to neglect any of life's possibilities—surrounded as they were by other musicians, facing the conductor (even suffering from his self-inflicted wounds, and who was now only illusorily leading the ensemble by frowning, puckering his lips, clicking his tongue, rolling his eyes, and twitching his nose), facing this large crowd of witnesses who weren't allowing one bit of the performance to escape them—decided that glancing at the music and playing the notes they deciphered was a possibility they would no longer resist, after having told themselves, over a period of time curiously equal to that of a faithful execution of the work from beginning to end, that they had exhausted all other options, so that, to the conductor's stupefaction—he was the only one excluded from this common impetus—the final chord bloomed with such concision that it seemed the obvious finale to a faithful performance of the work, which all of us would have then sworn we had attended.

A bit later Queene and I were back in our four-poster baldachin-style bed, which was our true home.

Queene proclaimed herself perfectly content that evening, in spite of . . . I believed her and felt perfectly happy.

THE OTHER SIXTUS

But, in order to discuss our carnal relations more accurately, perhaps I should have simply copied a few pages from the unearthed manuscript—but is it time yet?—even if I didn't recognize myself in the narrator, a solitary, sensuous ladies' man, even if the odd character named Sixtus couldn't be me for the obvious reason that I had never known any women before Queene and would never know any after. Whereas he, on the other hand . . .

Well, here it is.

". . . . ."

No, I realize that I can't. That my hand refuses to obey. All those crudely described copulations! All those details from some kind of sexual biography starting at birth: ("In the womb, the ultrasounds already showed a kind of little dirk attached to the fetus; and so remained my virile member, high and hard, for the rest of my life")! And that list of conquests, indifferently recalled, without cruelty, but with an insensitivity on the part of the hero whose only concern seemed to be making them c . . . in such a way that they'd never forget it, he didn't care about anything else: ("The most passionate onslaughts of their most adored lovers on the days of their most feral excitement would leave no stronger a mark on the women's memories than the lightest brush of a willow branch against their Gateway to Pleasure, when compared with the assaults of my wild and indefatigable monster, after which they shall remain beside themselves in ecstasy until their dying day")! And this narrative, too direct in its attempts to pull Queene—so sweet and beautiful, and who nevertheless loved me, I knew it, with a love as infinite as my own—from her frigidity ("Sweet nothings, delicate caresses, and precautious penetrations, nothing could vanquish her impassibility. The last week, from one dawn to the next, and every day after that—a flash of sunlight, which didn't always emanate from the sun itself but was occasionally reflected off the Sublima's rearview mirror even though it was parked under the interior garden's tall trees, would irritate my eye at times—I f . . . her incessantly, an arduous task interspersed with unparalleled ejaculations every three hours, and I would keep going, going, going, making the bed, the room, the whole house shake with each thrust; the onset of orgasmic spasms oft-times shook the Earth, but not Queene. I even believe that she became colder and colder each day, as if she were lifeless")!

No, I can't.

The final evening, without the slightest aforethought, I sat down in the immense office looking out onto the Calle de Margarita and

I tried once again to put down in writing the story of my adventures, this time successfully.

I must admit that I only recopied the manuscript.

There was no other way out.

Queene was sleeping.

VIII

MY CHILD

OUT OF REACH

"In other words, playing both sides and more than ever desirous of penetrating these indefinable appearances, be it even by some supreme artifice which would leave this indefinable ineffableness out of reach, alas, I started to move my head like a stubborn mule's, from left to right, right to left. These movements, by altering the direction of my vision, at this hour where nightfall continued to obscure my hand moving over the page (absorbed as I was in my work, I hadn't thought of turning on the lights in the spacious office), permitted me to see, as it were, the movement of several hands, whose bony extremities seemed to labor as one, together on the same stroke and scratch of pen on the page, repeated and increasingly brief, with no respite other than that of the single, real hand returning to its initial position, ever the more frequently—time was pressing, pressing!—so that eventually it was unnecessary for my eyes to wander in order to discern an ever-shortening stroke under a hand whose outline was dissipating bit by bit to the point of being invisible. But, I simply peered downwards as, at the same moment, perception vanished and the stroke diminished to nothing more than an immobile point—so that no action would ever again help me find in my head, or on paper, or in life what had been destroyed or had vanished."

I returned to the bedroom. Being careful not to stir Queene, I placed the two manuscripts, the one that was the fruit of my labor and the other, in my suitcase (an attractive, new suitcase that I had purchased, among a thousand other little things, the morning of our arrival), then I slipped in next to my beloved.

A CHILD OF QUEENE'S

A few hours later, on the morning of the final day, Queene confessed her incurable sorrow: her body, which was so beautiful, was barren. Would I have liked to have a child with her? "Yes." Would I abandon her? "No." What's more, I told her, I loved her with all my soul and I was sure that our love would forge a miracle.

"If not," she told me, "one day maybe we could kidnap a child, hold it for ransom and then keep the child and the ransom?"

My blood froze, colder than it had been even in Luc's hotel. Was she prepared to commit such a crime? So who was she then? I could imagine a thousand different stories, past and future, in which we were the protagonists. For example: one day someone kidnaps Queene, asks me for money and I never see her again, or perhaps: it was Queene's scheme from the beginning—but after how many tricks, ten, a hundred, a thousand!—she had eliminated Armelle and her abductor, she wanted a man (me) to love her and be her slave . . .

Kidnap a child? No, she swore that she was incapable of such a crime. But she was prepared to spin a thousand tales to keep me. I needed to be reassured: we were absolutely in our own story and no other. We had no other recourse than to wait for the ending.

PART TWO
DYING

(A NEW TESTAMENT)

.

I

THE ART OF MODELLING

FAKED DEATH

I decided to pass myself off as dead in Anita's eyes.

Why such an undertaking, so extraordinary, so seemingly cruel? Because there was no other way out. There was no other way out if I wanted our love to endure, by any means necessary.

Before explaining myself further and evoking the painful developments that led me to this act, I immediately wish to provide two pieces of information, so that their appearance does not bog down the story precisely when it should flow swiftly and steadily like water.

Here they are.

Firstly, I did not willingly believe in doppelgängers—hardly more, may I add, than in identical or Siamese twins. I believed in them because we have to, because we cannot deny what is, but something in me said no.

And yet, at the end of this story, I really and truly did encounter my doppelgänger, a man who seemed to be me, but wasn't.

KLEHR'S SYNDROME

Secondly, my cousin Marianne, the eldest of my aunt Blanca's four daughters, died at the age of nineteen from Klehr's Syndrome, a very rare congenital disorder culminating in a type of leukemia that leads to death within a few months (six, in my cousin's case). During the last months it is contagious through salivary secretions. Well-cleaned dishes are enough to keep others out of danger. On the other hand, all kissing is forbidden. That's the only real risk for contagion.

But I never kissed my cousin Marianne. We spent many an hour holed up in her little apartment on rue des Archers, in L. (not too far from the famed Hôtel-Dieu Hospital), chatting and listening to music (Tomás Luis de Victoria: after many years I even recall a singer's name, Annemicke Cantor, whose alto worked wonders in his famous *Missa sine nomine*), and many an hour strolling in L., for as long as Marianne's strength held up, my hand holding hers.

There was no other physical contact between us. And Klehr's Syndrome or not, there wouldn't have been any other contact. So it was a first love that endured the separation of two bodies, that even required it.

Starting in my adolescence, I would regularly model objects of various forms from plaster. They represented nothing specific and were always about two feet long at most. I'd model the fresh plaster (which remained so, thanks to a treatment of my own invention), until a precise moment when I'd consider it finished. Not that the object itself offered a real feeling of completion at that point—but I'd have had enough, and overcome with anxiety and nervousness, unable to continue, I'd feel compelled to stop—but for this reason, nonetheless, one could call it a finished work and not simply abandoned.

Over time I became quite adept, and noticed that these objects were receiving more and more attention. When people looked at them they found it hard to turn away. Soon buyers were seeking me out in ever-greater numbers, so that I no longer needed to worry about a career. My plaster works insured me a comfortable existence.

MIDLIFE

Later, at an age that could no longer be termed youth, after my parents' deaths and after my divorce from Anne-Marie, I sank into a period of acute torpidity of which I had already been a victim after the death of my cousin Marianne.

So many mortal wounds!

Alas, I was to receive many others. (But, cruel fate, one dies from these mortal wounds only after having received them all.)

What to do? The solution came from my friend Yves Somme, with whom I had passed many hours chatting on the telephone and who would visit me every time he returned to L.

I met Yves at the famous Lycée du Parc in L. It was there that our wonderful friendship blossomed and deepened over the course of the years. As disinterested as myself in the professions for which our studies were preparing us, he followed my example and devoted himself to the arts. First, painting appealed to him. He spent two years of his life reproducing scenes from Roman history with a facility of reproduction and meticulous attention to detail that made his canvases look like photographs. Then, following a quick conversion, he was drawn to sculpture and metalwork: he had found his calling. More knowledgeable in the ways of the world than I, he soon left for the capital—and it must be said, an artist of a different caliber than I—and quickly became quite well known. I found him extremely talented, in fact. He was a musician and played various instruments. He even composed short works for violin, flute, and guitar. Although academic in style, they were quite enjoyable to listen to.

Here's what he suggested to me: why not move into his apartment in Paris during his absence, which might be long term? (Indeed, he was having an intense affair with a Spanish woman, Manuela Narvaez—a classical musician, but also a flamenco dancer—and was preparing to join her in Madrid.) Perhaps the change would do me good, and I might feel like working again. (An astounding anecdote: this Manuela, when they first started living together, threatened to kill my old friend with a handgun during a fit of jealousy.)

Nothing but heartbreaking memories were keeping me in L. I accepted his offer.

BORN WITHOUT A FORWARDING ADDRESS

Fifteen days later (it was the 8th of January), fleeing my birthplace and tearing myself from my roots for the first time in my life (I, who abhorred leaving my neighborhood in Fourvière, even during summer), I went to live at Yves's place in Paris.

He had purchased a shop and the apartment above it from a merchant. It was on the corner of rue Manuel Dodelat and rue du Pasado Rey in the ninth arrondissement. On the second floor, the apartment comprised five rooms (including the kitchen), two looking out over rue Manuel Dodelat and three over rue du Pasado Rey, as well as the large shop on the ground floor, which Yves had made into his studio.

He had decorated the second floor himself. Which is to say that as soon as you opened the door you saw works worthy of a palace. Moreover, I had the pleasure of leisurely admiring some of my friend's older paintings (battle scenes, two self-portraits) and especially four recent sculptures, perfect collections of different metal parts—which seduced you with their feeling of complete achievement—one couldn't imagine other shapes, another combination—of solidity that defied time, but also of lightness and momentum. They were mature works, emancipated from the burden (and the moving sands) of their history. Gazing upon them calmed and liberated the mind—contrary to, you must understand, the sort of hypnotic imprisonment that would suddenly prompt me to stop kneading my plaster whirlwinds, saying to myself enough, enough.

The change was indeed beneficial. I took up sculpting again. Yves had given my name to thirty or so well-chosen people, and soon I was selling as many of my little sculptures as I had in L. What's more, some patrons stuck with me to the point of ordering pieces through the mail based on photographs I'd send them.

In February, Yves married the harpsichordist and dancer Manuela Narvaez. He invited me to his wedding, but unfortunately, extreme back pain prevented me from taking the trip.

Although he had moved to Madrid, he hadn't the least intention of selling his apartment in Paris, and I could, he told me, consider myself at home.

STRANGLEHOLD

I easily became accustomed to my new neighborhood. The hilly streets reminded me of Fourvière's terrain in L. (as they reminded Anita of the large hill in Croix-Rousse). Rue des Martyrs and rue Manuel Dodelat climbed, parallel, towards the Pigalle neighborhood. Rue du Pasado Rey was one of the numerous smaller streets that linked the two together.

One day, at the conclusion of a complicated story, whose purpose was to explain the street's new name and also to amuse Anita, I transformed rue des Martyrs into "Moo Day Raw Tears." Anita laughed openly, in a burst of childlike laughter that transformed her beautifully solemn face. And this laugh, which would suddenly make Anita so alive (whereas the gravity of her beautiful face seemed to ordain my death), would sometimes relax the stranglehold of anxiety that had squeezed my sides from the first day and continued during our entire relationship.

"Dodelat" easily became "Dotes-a-lot," "rue Dotes-a-lot."

We changed the street names.

Rue du Pasado Rey, very familiar to Spanish tourists, was first called rue du Passage du Roi, to celebrate the visit of King Philip IV of Spain to Paris in 1650.

THE PRIMARY SUBJECT OF HIS WORKS

In 1649, Diego Velázquez left Spain and undertook his second journey to Italy. Although he had a wife and children, he entered into a relationship with Anna Mori, a famous artist from Rome who made engraved metal medallions, some of which are still displayed at the Prado. (One of them depicted Velázquez himself.) In May 1651, the King summoned Velázquez, who was forced to return to Spain. Anna Mori was expecting.

At the end of 1651, Antonio, their son, was born in Rome, only shortly after the birth in Madrid of Philippe IV's daughter, Margarita.

So close and long-standing were the bonds between the king and his favorite painter, that Velázquez, faced with the impossibility of seeing his son, felt a real paternal love for the Infanta Marguerita. She became the primary subject of his last works.

When Velázquez was absent too long from Madrid, Philip IV missed him terribly. During these times the king allowed no one else to paint him. Eventually, he rather resolutely proclaimed, if it was not in fact an order, that Velázquez return. Deprived of his artist and confidant, who presented him with such a flattering image of himself, it was as if he were deprived of himself, of the best of himself. As for his duties as king, they bored him. He would occasionally travel to pass the time: thus he came to Paris in 1650. It was an official trip of course, but he really wished to visit a cousin, an old hunting companion, who, in his second marriage, had wed a French woman and was living in an immense residence where the current-day rue du Pasado Rey lies.

PASSION'S WAY

The residence was razed during the Revolution, and rue du Passage du Roi was no more.

Many years later, a secretly royalist civil servant of Spanish descent, and according to some a bit of a hothead, tried to impose a Spanish sounding variation of the original name, rue du Paso del Rey. He managed to do it, but died suddenly. Before the street signs were produced, the name continued through the bureaucratic chain, and misunderstood or miscopied, it metamorphosed into "Pasado Rey," "passed the king" or "the king passed."

Afterwards, as is frequently the case, the mistake was perpetuated.

Pretending to hear "passion's way" for "Pasado Rey," I started calling it "Passion's Way" in honor of Anita and our love.

My first three months of residence at Yves's (until his visit, at the beginning of March, and Anita's telephone call) passed quickly. The days, dedicated to work, were unchanging.

In the evenings I'd sit in the large living room on the second floor overlooking rue Dodelat and read. When I had difficulty concentrating on my reading I would lose myself in contemplation of one of Yves Somme's early works, which hung on the wall facing the sofa. Over a large area (2 x 3 meters), it depicted Spartacus's final battle against the Roman army in 71 B.C. The courage and repeated victories of the former Thracian shepherd and escaped slave had threatened Roman power for two years.

But this time he would be defeated.

Six thousand slaves were crucified along the Appian Way.

At the onset of the revolt, the slaves' intentions were not bellicose. They only wished to return to their original countries to live with their families. When Spartacus, who escaped from a gladiatorial school in Capua one summer's evening in 73 B.C. and who had already amassed seventy-four loyal followers, promised them they could return to their homes if they followed him, they followed him. Aided by the Gaul, Crixus, Spartacus was able to enlist nearly one hundred thousand men.

The odious Crassus prevailed. Slaves lie dying, crucified as far as the eye can see. Spartacus is in the foreground. Near death, he seems to be looking at us with his beautiful, dark eyes, made even darker by his mop of curly black hair. His noble yet desperate face in Yves Somme's painting is a masterpiece of mimetic art, as can be said of the entire work.

I would then go into the sitting room (looking out over Passion's Way) where I'd listen to music: Ranlequin de Mol, Loÿs Compère, Nicolas Gombert, Marbrianus de Orto, Costanzo Porta, Pierre de la Rue, Bartholomeo de Escobedo, Tomás Luis de Victoria, all the while thinking of my cousin Marianne.

Listening to these Renaissance voices at Yves's was an unparalled experience thanks to the quality of his stereo equipment—sound forged by the Sphinx Myth 9 compact disc player, fortified by the Audio Analogue R integrated amplifier, and disseminated by Adamentes III loudspeakers (whose lower frequencies were subtly extended by the Magnat Omega 380 subwoofer), without mentioning the Van den Hul "The First" and Synergistic Research Looking Glass interconnects and power cords.

How many hours must Anita and I have spent in front of the Adamentes IIIs, reveling in the music, music that didn't seem to come from electronic circuits and transducers, so pure and natural was it.

Joy of joys, the more real the musical reproduction seemed, the deeper we found ourselves in an unreal and magical world: indeed, that all of these singers seemed present in the room to this extreme point (you only really needed to close your eyes to see them), was hardly believable, or possible, or real. We could hear the voices, we were no longer on Earth, we were living with the spirits.

"How are you, you little glow worm?" Yves said to me (so, beginning of March) on walking through the doorway.

Ha, ha! The old "little glow worm" from our schooldays had survived the decades.

We warmly embraced one another.

"Better, thanks to you . . ."

We spent the day chatting. He showed me some photos of Manuela, his wife, a beautiful and fierce-looking Spaniard (particularly beautiful and fierce-looking dressed as a flamenco dancer in the photograph of a canvas Yves had painted based on a photograph), of her parents, Aurelio (a high-ranking officer in the Spanish army) and Mariquita Narvaez, who both looked very old, and finally of the mansion in the heart of a park just west of Madrid where they lived—a mansion whose doors were always open to me, of course. (But on more than one occasion I had the feeling that Yves preferred to visit me alone in Paris. I would not learn why until later—too late, alas!)

It was in the corridors of this mansion that Manuela pulled a gun on him one night. A fit of jealousy. She was jealous of his romantic past. Luckily, this only happened once, and the most perfect harmony reigned between them from then on.

Yves, who had Spanish blood from his mother, greatly enjoyed Madrid. He lived in luxury and opulence and had found in Manuela, of this he was sure, his soul mate. Yet, I believed I could detect that his general demeanor, in spite of his claims of perfect contentment, had darkened. I had occasionally gotten an inkling of this during our phone conversations, and on seeing him I was sure of it. I asked him about it, but he didn't know what to say.

He hadn't noticed anything. He didn't feel any different. And I myself was unable to explain it any more precisely.

He congratulated me on my latest pieces, which were quite accomplished in his opinion. As for me, I didn't see any difference, other than that I was stopping the sculpting process earlier and earlier, that I became weary more quickly, even overwrought, and following the particular criteria I had decided on, I considered them finished sooner.

That evening I accompanied Yves back to the airport in a taxi, where we said goodbye with our usual warm feelings.

ANITA *or* THE FOURTH ANGEL

I had just returned to rue du Pasado Rey when the phone rang. It was Anita M., a quite young woman from L. Having finished her degree in art history, she earned a living writing for several publications and was currently working on an article about me: would I be willing to meet her?

I accepted.

I believe that everything is contained in the first moment. It didn't occur to me to refuse, whereas I believe I would have said no to anyone else.

She knocked on my door the following Monday at 5:30, holding a black leather briefcase. Black also were her beautiful eyes and her long hair whose ends curled.

We spoke for two and a half hours.

I was touched by a little speech impediment she had, endearing in the way that something which escapes human control and so becomes more animal-like is endearing, as touching as a sneezing puppy or a stumbling lamb is touching—a way of pronouncing words that palatalized and softened certain letters, such as *s* or *g*, and really more or less every sound.

When she left I felt she was taking my life away in her black briefcase. Should I have asked her not to leave and to stay with me, composing her article while I modeled my plaster?

What to do?

Thorns of anxiety were already pricking my head and stomach.

J.-S.B., A.B., F.M.-B.

I called her the same evening, as soon as she had arrived in L.

When she opened the door to her little apartment in the Croix-Rousse neighborhood, the phone rang. It was I.

I phoned her again the following day, then again, and every day after that.

She was as confident and fearful as a baby. She listened to music constantly. She only liked J.-S.B., A.B., and F.M.-B., three angels if one paid close attention, she always said. How quickly I came to love her, how quickly I adored Anita!

Two months passed.

We telephoned one another everie nyght, without really alluding to seeing each other again, but both of us knowing that through these increasingly long and intimate discussions we were perfecting the moment of our reunion—and one mid-May nyght, I suggested that she move in with me at Yves Sommes's place on the corner of rue Manuel Dodelat and rue Pasado Rey.

She came.

All she left behind her was one friend, Alecta.

But what a friend!

Anita and Alecta had known each other since childhood and loved one another like sisters. They spent a great deal of time together. Anita had even lived with Alecta for over a year in a little house in Villeurbanne that Alecta had inherited from her parents.

But Paris and L. are close. Alecta, a stage actress, frequently crossed the country to perform here and there, and they could always phone.

I I

ANITA

NOT YET WRITTEN

My raven-haired and fearful Anita (she was afraid of wind, cars, illness, afraid of everything) resided for eight months at rue Dodelat, eight months during which the distance between us was never more than a few feet, if you exclude the five brief trips she made to Alecta's in L., an hour and a half spent at the dentist's on rue de Maubeuge ("Moon Fudge") for the removal of a painful molar, and several afternoons in a library consulting some art books that she was unable to find at the specialty bookstore on rue de Châteaudun ("Dung Chateau"), a pretentious bookstore whose employees acted like royalty and would not accept the idea that they didn't have the book you were seeking ("If it's not here, it has not yet been written")—because after the success of her article on my plaster work, Anita was very much in demand and was working a great deal, whereas I on the other hand worked less and less as the months passed. This increased my anxiety and made me agonize over my situation even more, as if my soul, deprived of the nourishment that I had always given it through sculpture, was now ruthlessly taking it out on me with an insatiable force.

SYLVIE DAUMAL

One day while Anita was away, a redhead, Sylvie Daumal, knocked on my studio door. From Anita's article she knew where I worked, but had not found my name in the telephone directory (because it wasn't there). Eager to acquire one of my works, she had taken the liberty of . . .

About forty years old, well-dressed, beautiful, attractive (but need I make it clear that I wasn't in the least attracted to her?), I learned that she was a clinical biologist and was the director of a medical testing lab near Rumilly in Upper Savoy. She came to Paris from time to time to meet colleagues, attend conventions, and, an art lover, visit museums and shows.

She had a plethora of magazine subscriptions. In Anita's article she had seen photographs of the plasters and a photograph of the artist. I quickly suspected—and she didn't try to conceal this—that her interest centered as much on the plaster sculptor as on the plaster itself. For my part, while being infinitely delicate about it I didn't conceal the fact that for all women bar one, I was unavailable. Having thus defined the nature of our relationship, and Sylvie having accepted it with surprising yet profound kindness—we had the pleasure of discussing sculpture and Velázquez, her favorite painter. (At least once a year she would visit the Prado Museum in Madrid.)

She picked out a plaster work: "The last one," she said.

She handed me her card, just in case I happened to be in the area one day ("Sylvie Daumal, Couty Medical Laboratory, Sales (Couty), Rumilly, Upper Savoy"), and she left. She had parked her Toyota SUV on the sidewalk, almost in front of my door. She loved to drive, she told me, and she loved her SUV.

THE REST OF THE WORLD

Anita and I lived like recluses.

Only one time—one time in nearly three quarters of a year!—did we spend just over thirty minutes in a café on rue des Martyrs ("Moo Day Raw Tears").

Our love story reduced the rest of the world to nothing. But now, my Anita, I know today (today!) our story was nothing other than the world without *us*.

We toil relentlessly to hide beneath artifice that which is naturally out of reach.

How do you leave yourself? How do you enter yourself? With Anita present, I was freed from everything that I was, from everything that I was not.

At night I would watch her sleep. She would hold my right hand, and my left would be on her shoulder, or her hair, and these moments with her, in the silence of rue du Pasado Rey, were the best of my life, more precisely, the only ones, yes, the only moments of my life.

I would never again know them.

I would never again hear Anita's laugh.

What happened after this "never again," I wouldn't know until after-after.

But let's wait.

DOMESTIC LIFE

When she was speaking at length with Alecta, Anita would draw primitivist portraits of herself with colored pencils on a sheet of paper by the phone.

Occasionally, she would playfully claim that my lower teeth were too small, which was untrue.

We would refer to Yves Somme as "Simone."

The words that we transmogrified became more and more numerous, tightening the circle of irreality in which we had imprisoned ourselves from the very first day a little more, an irreality that had expanded when we talked for centuries on the phone, and which would continue to expand after Anita's return to L., when we would once again talk for centuries on the phone.

(I have no hesitation in measuring the time of our love story in centuries: after light came light, after night, night.)

In short, an irreality that didn't dissipate during our eight months of domestic life together, quite to the contrary. In less than two-and-a-half months (an incalculable number of centuries), two months and eleven days—I can precisely situate the event: mid-July, forty-eight hours before Yves Somme's second visit—we succeeded in uniting ourselves by the most unbreakable mental and corporeal bond that had ever united two people on this Earth, in imprisoning ourselves in a circle of infinite love which, at the moment it closed forever (after these two months and eleven days), resonated in our heads with a massive silent click.

Now, this circle of love melded inside me with a circle of anxiety that was forever closed: my God, why? Why?

DRESS REHEARSAL OR YVES'S TALES

That is the question I attempted to elucidate, in mid-July, with the help of my friend Yves. We spent nearly three hours in the sitting room while Anita was curled up in the ground-floor studio writing a long article on the latest works of Philippe Deroux, the famed maker of "vegetable peel collages" from Villeurbanne.

Yves freed me from the tenebrous labyrinth of my questions and hypotheses. I had so frequently enumerated the basic elements of the problem during our phone conversations, and he had reflected so thoroughly on the situation that his analysis seemed to be a clear, logical, and abstract summary of my current situation with Anita.

ONE LIFE TOO MANY

If Anita wanted my life so badly (he told me), *well, that meant that she herself wasn't living. There was no doubt that by her very nature she embodied desire, possibility; she was but a receptacle for life. Now if this theft were so easy, logically, it was because my own life—from the moment of my birth, if I paid close attention and looked back on my past systematically—was ripe for the picking, as if floating within me, without really living in me, simply affecting to animate me (having forever pretended to be alive, I could, of course, unwittingly model one more tormented plaster work). And so, this life was condemned to find a lifeless home one day—Anita—in order to finally play its swansong, to make someone—Anita—live and consequently to give me a feeling of life, at least while it left, moved in, and settled elsewhere!*

Thus we were but one person, Anita and I.

But what then? Yes, what then? Tomorrow, over the following days and weeks, over the months that would follow, over the coming centuries? If Anita remained attached to me and if this transfusion of life continued in this manner even though my life was no longer in me but in her—if the movement of appropriation and loss, combined with such infinite violence and obstination that it henceforth seemed like a perpetual-motion machine operating outside of our bodies, controlling us without seeking our accord, if this movement endured, implacably and perpetually, as it had already thus endured over the last twenty-four hours, although it should have stopped once the theft had been perpetrated—under these conditions, why wouldn't it continue forever, for we were well on our way!—but then what part of my being could she extract from me, if it were no longer life, and through what suffering? Yes, unimaginable and unending torment threatened me, torment that would shock Satan himself!

(Alas, Yves was not incorrect. Between the day before his visit and the 4th of January the following year, the day Anita left for

L., I was reduced to a knot of misery and dread, to a clenched fist, mine, in which I was crushing myself, and whose grip soon restricted all movement, such that the only resistance I offered to this evil was a corpse's invulnerability.)

What to do? Yves related it to me in his second treatise.

ABDOMENS

If the bond could not be broken (so he started), *if it were starving me while feigning to feed me, if it were destroying me while becoming itself more and more indestructible, my options were extremely limited: to escape the debacle, there was a honed blade, nicked and reddened, that was being handed to me. I had to scratch out my eyes so as not to suffer the ghastly spectacle of my empty eye sockets—and, my hands severed, I was forced to model the very story of this mutilation with plaster!*

What to do?

The solution—imperfect and perhaps not definitive—was cruel yet unavoidable: as soon as I could muster the courage, quickly, while there was still time, I must distance myself from Anita forever!

We could start to phone one another again, but we would no longer see one another. The bond would endure, less and less alive, but less and less deadly. I would be like an aeronaut, still far from his destination, yet dumping his ballast: if he doesn't wish to crash into the mountain face, or take a nose dive into the deep sea, he must resolve to sacrifice his extremities, to cut off his arms and legs and throw them overboard. Which is quite challenging for the last arm (Yves added jokingly, as if to remind me of our crazy laughter during school, those laughs that were almost life-threatening, so tightly were our abdomens contracted, so viciously was our breath cut short). *He suggested that I start immediately, joint by joint, finger by finger.*

To entreat Anita, my beloved, to return to L., our home town! To never see her again! Was this death?

Yves begged my pardon for his distressing advice. Pardon for what? He perfectly upheld his role as a friend, and for that I thanked him heartily.

Then, in an effort to escape the oppressive weight that had overtaken me, I quickly said to him, simply to change the subject of our discussion, something that just crossed my mind:

"That chest of drawers is a jewel!"

A MYSTERY

I indicated a small, dark, well-patinaed Andalusian piece of furniture made from thick wood underneath the window.

"That's the same word I used, a jewel, when I saw it in Manuela's mansion," Yves told me, "the first time I went to Madrid. A few days after my return to Paris—think of what a treasure she is, see how much she loves me!—a trucking company delivered the chest. Did you look in the lower drawer?"

The question surprised me.

"No, why?"

"The drawer was locked, and the key lost. When Aurelio Narvaez purchased the mansion, about thirty years ago, the chest was there, with its bottom drawer locked. I managed to open it. Look at what I discovered. No name. The writing is illegible."

He handed me a thick notebook bound in red leather, which was worn. Old photographs had been affixed to the first few pages. They were followed by a hand-written piece of music that had no title (the first notes of which I hummed to myself). Next were approximately thirty pages filled with what was indeed terrible handwriting. You couldn't make out one word. Besides the fact that the ink had faded, the letters were too small or large, too stretched out or too squat, and the lines weren't straight, rising, falling, undulating, and looping back around on themselves. The only legible parts were the numerals I and II at the top of two pages, which seemed to indicate two chapters, two parts, two stories, it was impossible to know, and the numeral III, the final graphical indication of the manuscript at the top of a blank page. There were only white pages after that point, or rather yellowish gray ones.

INVESTIGATION

During another stay in Madrid, Yves had played the short piece on Manuela's incredible harpsichord with its three keyboards, a Bartolomeo Cristofori from 1721. Manuela had immediately recognized *Bonita* ("Pretty Girl"), a composition for guitar from the very first collection of a Spanish composer of the lowest rank, Miguel Padilla (1899–1956).

With this element deciphered thanks to Manuela's erudition (a musician who was capable of playing a large part of J.-S.B.'s works for clavier by heart), it was easy to continue the investigation. A chemical analysis of the ink indicated a gap of at least two years between the copying of the composition and the writing on the following pages. Now, during the last months of his life, Miguel Padilla was stricken with a degeneration of the nervous system whose symptoms, among others, included terrible shaking over his entire body. He spent these last months of his life in the mansion that Aurelio Narvaez would buy many years later and in which Yves and Manuela lived today.

The red notebook, therefore, was a sort of personal scrapbook abandoned by Padilla once he had placed the photographs (of both himself and his parents) and *Bonita* inside, which he decided to take up again after the disease struck him so devastatingly. He wrote as well as he could, in spite of the shaking, a few pages under the heading I, others under II—God only knows to say what—then he had to give it up after having valiantly inscribed the numeral III.

And he put the notebook away in the chest's lower drawer.

Such was the simple story of Miguel Padilla's red notebook.

PLOT TWIST

Yves put the notebook back in its drawer.

"You'll really have to excuse me for earlier," he said, getting up.

I walked towards him and gave him a hug. I think he was ready to cry. Yves really cared for me. I also believe today (today!) that he wanted to talk to me, to tell me something at that very moment about himself, and that he held himself back. I don't know. Perhaps I'm imagining things. Perhaps I'm imagining given what happened the following year and the letter he sent me at that time: the following year, at the beginning of June, in the Madridian mansion where weapons filled every room, Yves Somme killed his wife Manuela and himself.

III

THE NARVAEZ REPORT

WHY?

Anita drifted off to sleep like an angel.

Not me. I tossed and turned until the early hours, afflicted as I was by Yves's visit and haunted by the first notes of Padilla's piece, which refused to leave my head.

At dawn I fell into some sort of dream.

At the end of a long road I arrived in front of the Narvaez residence, a vast, one-story rectangular building located in the heart of a large, empty area. The setting sun was dazzling, reflecting off thousands of window panes. It was very hot. I was a journalist, like Anita, but I didn't completely understand why I was there, why I had been offered such an assignment, nor why I had accepted. I who rarely left the city limits, let alone the confines of my apartment, drew material for my articles from books and never working on location.

The old and formidable Aurelio Narvaez had wanted a journalist from the city to witness the birthday party of his daughter Manuela and to write an account of it for the newspaper. I was to arrive at dusk. After dinner, there would be a concert. Then, I could rest for a few hours in a bedroom reserved for me and leave at daybreak. My task was to record the events of the party, minute by minute. I should always have my quill and notebook in hand: the more I was seen writing, the better.

Alecta, my editor, had phoned me at noon.

"But why me?"

"Narvaez himself requested you. The paper will pay you a fortune!"

HELP!

The doorknocker rapped against the door. A guard opened the double doors. The large, interior courtyard, packed with guests, was brightly lit. Three staircases gave access to the second-floor gallery. On my right were long tables that had already been set, on my left a stage was being prepared for the musicians. No one, except the cadaverous majordomo, paid any attention to me. He wanted to introduce me to Aurelio Narvaez. Seeking, but not finding him, he led me to my room on the second floor.

We walked along the gallery. The door to one of the rooms opened. A young, blond woman exited, followed by two men.

"Manuela!" whispered the majordomo.

How beautiful she was! How beautiful was Aurelio Narvaez's late-born, sickly, and only daughter! Sick? Yes, from a mysterious disease, a languorous state that precluded any strong or prolonged effort.

The old man who was following her—Aurelio Narvaez!—had a deeply wrinkled face and I was frightened by his extreme state of exhaustion. I wouldn't have been surprised if he had dropped dead on the spot.

"The Master of the house!" whispered the majordomo. Come, come pay both of them your respects . . .

The old slave driver looked at me as if I didn't exist, as if he saw no part of me, except, perhaps, the notebook clutched against my chest. And perhaps he muttered a thank you for my presence there.

Manuela's attitude was completely different. She held my hand in hers while we exchanged greetings—and I could discern some distress in her gaze, like a cry for help: "Save me, save me!" she seemed to scream silently. From what? There was no time for explanations. But, with a squeeze of my hand and a knowing glance, I intimated to her that I understood her call.

In my room, I took a long bath, which was absolutely necessary after the journey in this torrid climate. I took a moment to put the details of my arrival at the Narvaez residence down in writing and then went to dinner, notebook under my arm.

THE EXECUTIONER

The majordomo sat me at my table, a table far from the others, small and round, a single table where no one would talk to me, nor look at me, nor perhaps even see me—with the exception of

Manuela, whose dark eyes met mine a thousand times over the course of the evening—and a thousand times I had to restrain myself from getting up and going over to her, judging the act too dangerous. (In my dream I deduced that I shouldn't undertake this imprudent action.)

An inedible meal is what I recorded in my notebook. Was the meal different, in spite of appearances, from the one served to the other guests? And why did I sense a feeling of hostility directed toward me? A crazy idea? In any case, the appetizer arrived. I had great difficulty prying it off the plate, where it must have been placed sometime during the Middle Ages. And a hail of bullets from the most powerful weapon would have ricocheted off the meat they served me next, the bullets' shapes reduced to solid stains of varying forms, unless, ill-at-ease, they decided to live out the rest of their slug-like days as one with the lettuce leaf that lay fearfully next to the meat, and which the slightest puff of air could dislodge, blowing this large fringe of grayish corruption far off into the distance.

And yet the other guests were rolling their eyes back in their heads and smacking their lips to show their gastronomical satisfaction.

Was someone attempting to poison me?

Yes, a crazy idea, an idea from a bad dream, a dream that Anita's fears had definitely tainted. She loved to eat, but was very frequently afraid that her food was contaminated and would kill her.

I made the careless mistake, in trying to swallow this dreadful food, of downing an entire glass of thick, dark, velvety-looking wine. A grave mistake. At first, I remained alarmingly impassive, as if I were lost in intense reflection. Then I started to shake. My face became covered in yellow spots, two long jets of a kind of rusty vapor whistled out of my nose, my hair shot out like sunbeams around my face, my ears folded over and wildly struck my temples, and my eyes, popping out of their orbits like two twitching cylinders, looked at one another, stunned, then, as though frightened, headed quickly and painfully back to their rightful places. Finally, my entire body started to spasm, assailed as it was by strong internal gasses, which my buccal cavity could only expel in the form of calamitous eructations, a kind of modulating din that forged an arduous passage from the depths of my being and made my lips undulate irregularly, producing the illusion of a unknown language whose delivery was so rapid it seemed as if I was begging for my life to be saved, explaining myself, justifying an infinitely complex problem point by point, while the executioner had already raised his axe.

SIXTE

The musicians played a series of variations on a simple theme (from Miguel Padilla!), but their hearts weren't in it. One might have even thought that they had never played in their entire lives, or had forgotten everything they knew about music. As for the conductor, Luc So-and-so, he had no control over them and only managed to injure himself when his movements became too imperious.

The evening came to an end.

Queene (her name was now Queene, or Anita—yes, it was Anita, it was she!—and not Manuela), Queene left, exhausted, almost being carried out by two servants.

From the gallery she gazed at me one last time. It was like a final call, help me, save me!

But perhaps I was imagining things. I too headed back to my room. Knowing that I wouldn't be able to sleep, I endeavored to compile my notes concerning the meal and concert.

An hour later, someone knocked lightly on my door. I opened it. It was Queene's lady companion. She seemed frightened.

"I hope no one saw me!" she said in a hushed voice. "My mistress asked me to take you to her room, if you wish. But we must be careful, very careful!"

I followed her straight away.

Alas, two men were waiting for us in the gallery. One was holding a pistol. He struck the poor servant with a sudden and sickening brutality. I understood the situation. I knew his job was to eliminate me. I quickly grabbed his arm and turned the weapon back towards him at the precise moment that he pulled the trigger, while with my right leg I kicked the other man over the balustrade.

I quickly returned to my room to get my coat, notebook, and pen and set out to find Queene.

AN ODD ESCAPE

I walked along the gallery. Carefully peering around a corner, I saw a huge detachment of armed men guarding Queene's door. I had no choice but to escape, if I could, that is—vacate the premises, head home, and come back with reinforcements!

I walked down one of the staircases. The courtyard was deserted. There wasn't a sound. Nevertheless, I carried on, like a shadow hugging the walls.

I then walked by my second attacker. He was definitely more fragile than he seemed initially, and the fall had been a hard one: the impact had turned him into a kind of black pool, in which a torn ear, two shards of nasal cartilage, an eye, and some teeth floated, moved by the whims of the evening breeze.

I made it to the double door without incident. Luckily the guard was sleeping so I wouldn't be delayed by another fight. Before leaving the building, I thought that perhaps the guard was dreaming this entire story of a chronicler from the city, in which case a good kick to the ribs would wake him—and would wake me too, in my bed!

But I remained prudent and slipped out through the heavy, half-open doors.

I closed them.

No chance of going back now. The world seemed to me like a vast prison.

Dawn was breaking.

I was surprised that my car, my beautiful Sublima S 24, wasn't parked next to the exterior wall. Then I forgot my surprise.

I wanted to run. I rushed out, propelled by an irresistible desire to run away from the Narvaez residence, to save my life and Queene's too, to bring back reinforcements from a far-away city . . .

But I didn't run. On the contrary, I walked slowly. I walked along the side of the huge building and tried to locate Queene–Manuela's room . . . This one . . . ? No, that one! Yes, it had to be that one.

My pen and notebook would hinder my short ascent. I threw them over my shoulder and started to climb, humming the theme and meager variations from the odd concert a few hours beforehand.

With great effort I hoisted myself up to the second floor. Queene was alone in her room. She saw me. She arose from her bed, smiled, and opened her arms—then she froze with a look of mingled hope and terror on her face, unable to move, to come to me, to open the window, doubtlessly too fatigued from her illness—and she started to scream, scream, I saw her screaming!

I didn't hesitate: with my clenched fist I broke the window, bam! drriiingg!

The sound of the breaking glass continued on, then stopped, then restarted, then stopped . . .

"It's Alecta," said Anita, getting out of bed.

It was indeed Alecta on the phone. She and Anita spoke for a long time, as always. Alecta would soon be coming to Paris. She didn't know exactly when, but soon.

IV

FAKED DEATH

LIFE

What flowed out of our thousands of wounds between July and January had to be called "life," Anita's and mine.

SINGING YOURSELF HOARSE IN A VIOLIN

As for my efforts to stop the hemorrhaging, they were useless. It was like singing into a violin, they only precipitated our fall.

SLOWLY BUT SURELY

Jealousy was the first spectacular sign of our disaster. It overcame us during the second half of July: Anita was suddenly troubled by the chaste relationship that had brought my cousin Marianne and me together years ago. During a night of tears, anger, and distress, she even mentioned the possibility that I see a doctor to ensure that I didn't have Klehr's Syndrome, and that I wasn't slowly but surely killing her with someone else's disease. I calmly explained to her (at least a thousand times, she was beside herself) that I couldn't have Klehr's Syndrome, that nothing was more impossible.

And I beseeched her—inasmuch as I was absolutely certain: she completely understood that I was ready to do anything to please her, ready to confront an army of executioners, a smile on my lips as the axe fell—I beseeched her to not insist that I undergo the long and painful medical testing, which was the only way to obtain an absolute diagnosis. In fact, obtaining this required a dozen or so days of preparation (pills of all kinds, shots to change one's blood make-up and dye certain organs), to which was added a day and a half in the hospital for blood tests, x-rays, samples, etc.

Not to mention, I added, the dangers that close contact with the medical profession represented, in my opinion. Radiation, needles, and feeding tubes sparked and perpetuated the worst diseases on Earth (but not Klehr's Syndrome, my beloved).

HEALING

My final argument (during that evening's crisis) was that a healer of my caliber was protected from all diseases, an argument that didn't fail to touch my solemn but childlike Anita. I must say that

I frequently healed her from all sorts of afflictions. Admittedly, she was never sick. But she suffered from fear, from her imagination, from relapses that amplified and prolonged the slightest pain that fleetingly passed. So it was easy for me to drive out the sources of evil through the laying on of hands and the incantation of magic formulas, which transmitted my ardent healing will.

I thus cured my Anita from several ear infections, moments of blindness, numerous cases of food poisoning, a kidney tumor, which was nevertheless quite advanced, as well as paralysis in her right ankle, which had threatened to overtake her whole body if I hadn't put a stop to it. (And so I used to rub her stomach for many an hour in order to alleviate the quite real pain that her period would cause—heavy, irregular periods, so incredibly irregular that they became a kind of menace whose potential for pain constantly weighed on her.)

Alas, the sickness that my gifts as a healer couldn't vanquish was the one that was killing us, that killed us more and more with each month that went by, digging thousands of diabolical tunnels under the edifice of our love, devouring the depths of our happiness from the inside out, and each day preparing more ardently to rip out its heart.

ALECTA: IT'S ALL A CHARADE

Alecta stayed twice for three days, in August and then in November. She had discovered her calling: mime. In August she was accepted by the famed Mikhail, a Russian who had recently moved to Paris and who enraptured people with his ability to imitate incredibly varied situations—a whale hunt, a difficult child delivery, a military battle, playing all the roles and transmogrifying himself in an astounding way. In November, Mikhail (who was also big-hearted) was pleased with Alecta's progress and encouraged her to perform solo—if her chronic asthma would allow it, for Alecta had suffered from severe asthma since childhood.

Alecta's first stay on the corner of rue Dotes-a-Lot and Passion's Way brought a bit of relief to Simone's place. Anita's childhood friend, as blonde as Anita was raven haired, treated us to an evening of mime. It was absolutely magical to see her transform into Anita, or into myself, or even, crouching down and contorting herself on the living room rug, to suddenly become one of my modeled plaster works.

Alecta's second stay, at the end of November, was less joyful. Tension was tearing Anita and me apart. And Alecta, who was scheduled to perform at a mime festival in Nemours, was fighting her stifling condition. Her asthma, she said, wanted to prevent her from performing.

One night we thought she was going to die.

She and Anita spent a great deal of time together. I wonder if Alecta encouraged her to leave, to separate herself from the agony we were enduring.

BRAKE PADS

I was giving my life to Anita, even though I no longer had one, according to the deductions and conclusions so well expressed by Yves, just as we sometimes continue to apply the brakes even when the brake pads are gone. Thus, we wreck, we ruin, we sacrifice something that isn't designed for such a purpose or for such pressure (without mentioning the inescapable accident await-ing us). The comparison, while seemingly striking and correct, might appear ill-chosen. Yet, it came quite naturally to me, since I've always loved cars. In my youth, I was a fast and skillful driver, perhaps the fastest and most skilled in the whole world.

LIFE'S JOURNEY

Of life's journey, one might say that the obstacle is insurmount-able and still out of sight. Yet it seemed to me that the obstacle would soon appear, and I was falling prey to this horror.

YEAR'S END

Thus the year drew to a close.

JANUARY 4TH

On January 4th Anita, succumbing to the desperate logic ac-cording to which we needed to feign separation in order to ex-haust and defeat this evil—then it would naturally leave us, so to speak—gathered her belongings and returned to L.

Within the heartbreaking situation in which we found our-selves, this final cut was hardly even noticeable, as if we were going to see each other that evening or the following day. We didn't believe it. It was the illusion of a bad dream—more so for Anita who only suffered from my own suffering (the only disease I may have actually transmitted to her during our time together)—and who did experience a brief moment of elation before her departure (such occurrences are not rare at the heart of the worst disasters): a return to L. would eliminate the evil that separated us; it was a means of staying close.

Once the evil had abated (quite soon, very quickly), she would return, and that would be that.

QUICK FLASH-FORWARD, I

But these mental constructions, these fragile cathedrals of fog, soon dissipated, and reality unfolded according to my worst fears. Exiled on a faraway planet, enjoined not to call me but once per century, Anita, in spite of herself and in spite of me, would have continued to sap what I had less and less of each day.

At the beginning of April I had a revelation of sorts: I understood that what I needed to mime, if we wished to retain a glimmer of hope, was not separation, but death itself.

I thus resolved to stage my own death for an audience of one, Anita, my beloved.

There was no other way out.

THE DEPARTURE

The taxi arrived via Passion's Way.

I kissed Anita, the passion of my life.

She stepped back and gazed at me with her sweet and imploring look: "Don't leave me, I beg of you, don't leave me!" That's what her eyes and her entire being were saying to me while trembling, even though her beloved lips were closed.

She was shaking. Her hands were shaking.

She climbed into the taxi. I could only see the dark hair on the back of her head and then, one last time, I caught a glimpse of her face when she turned around to wave goodbye, and then the car drove off.

I almost need to whisper to the reader, "Just a second. I'm going off to die and then I'll be back." So he'll at least allow me to go cry my eyes out in the next room before joining him again.

EVERIE NYGHT

Our telephone conversations recommenced, everie day, endlessly, everie nyght, and when I managed to fall asleep, Anita was even more present. I would watch her sleeping in my dreams,

> Since thus the night is worthie to me more
> And since I possess goode only through dreames,
> Slumber by day, Oh mine eyes, so poore!
> So that I may without ceasing dreame,

and so, as fleetingly as a dream, days and weeks flew by. I only recall a thousand jolts of life which killed me a thousand times over; I am talking of the thousands of times when I was on the brink of telling Anita what she hoped to hear every second: come back, my dear, now, immediately, I love you too much, forgive me!

Forgive me.

One line for this "forgive me" alone, it's not too much. Oh, no. It's not too much for this expression, forgive me. It seems to delineate the contours of my soul on paper, so frequently did I utter it, every second and with all my soul.

Yes, how many times—a thousand—barely out of the shower (holy terror of bathrooms, too much water), dressed in a robe, telephone in hand, my finest clothes, my finest watch, my finest ring laid out next to me on the couch, I would dial her number, ready to ask her to return immediately, right now—but, as soon as I heard her sweet and imploring voice, I spoke of everything except seeing each another again.

Forgive me, Anita, my angel, forgive me!

ANITA'S REBELLION

Then came the month of March.

Suddenly, Anita's suffering was no longer the passive reflection of my own suffering. She showed me great hostility, but a hostility that was unlike her—a purely invented hostility created to aid her in the battle that I had imposed upon her. In love with, yet separated from me, if she didn't retaliate, she risked death from the blows with which I was pummeling her, whereas by brandishing her invisible weapon, she could save a part of herself, and therefore a part of our love, albeit only in her imagination, and at what a price!

I continued in this way to sacrifice my life for Anita! And all the absurdities that still lay in wait for us were destined, in spite of all appearances, to prevent its death.

But at what a price!

But perhaps the reader, weary of these insinuations and explanations that dissolve as soon as you think you've grasped them, might wish, without any further ado, that something more elementary and real be placed in front of his eyes, or in his mouth, even in his hands, so that he may model it following his own desires.

Here it is.

FORGER

So Anita returned to her original line of attack—Klehr's Syndrome. Compelled to injure me for our mutual well-being, she demanded that I be tested. As I was no longer at her side to reassure and heal her, she had become frightened. Only an official document . . .

Otherwise, she would stop speaking to me. She would no longer answer the telephone.

Violent arguments broke out between the two of us (arguments between Anita and me!), which both separated and united us more than ever. Her threatening demand played an important part in our tale, obviously. But that I truly undergo, in the state that I was then in, this crucifixion by clinical testing I already mentioned—I mean undergo it for no real reason—Anita couldn't want it for too long, otherwise she would no longer be Anita, otherwise she would no longer be the Anita who comprehended with certainty the thousands of deaths I would have willingly suffered to save one single hair on her head—otherwise she would destroy herself and us.

One needed only wait: Anita was Anita.

Then it became impossible to wait.

How could I both do what she demanded and not do it?

I had an idea.

I ran it by Yves. He approved and nearly managed to obviate the scruples that the plan raised.

One morning I phoned Sylvie Daumal, the beautiful, red-headed biologist from Couty. She was happy to hear from me. She herself had wanted to call me several times, she told me, but hadn't been so bold. I confided that I had an ulterior motive and immediately described my situation.

Thanks to Sylvie, to her understanding, to her composure, to her kindness, everything was sorted out.

And so we became forgers, even if we didn't make public use of our forgery: Sylvie easily procured a piece of official letterhead from a Parisian clinic where one of her friends worked, reporting thereupon that I had tested negative, normal, perfect.

One more little lie was necessary for my plan to be perfectly executed, so that Anita, horrified, would not suddenly believe she was no longer Anita: new methods for diagnosing Klehr's Syndrome, which were rapid and simple, had been perfected. The plan was complete.

I didn't have Klehr's Syndrome, and consequently neither did Anita. With this artificial obstacle removed, a lull of several hours followed, also just as inevitably artificial, then—inevitably—the war recommenced with renewed vigor.

By mid-April, I could no longer defer the final blow and therefore had to partake in the most bitter of victories: simulating my own death.

I phoned Yves in Madrid.

But I wonder: might some people doubt that there was no other way out? And might they criticize me for the pain I would inflict on Anita—a pain she might possibly not survive, a pain she might even be tempted to curtail with an act, which, for her would not be simulated, etc.? To these accusers, dim-witted and cold-hearted, in my opinion unworthy to read this account, unworthy even to have eyes, I will nonetheless offer three responses.

First, a logical argument. The trap in which Anita and I were struggling would no longer allow us to survive: we were dying. In the throes of agony, I was readying myself to break this trap—even if we didn't survive. Secondly, knowing Anita as I did—and they should understand that the smallest molecule on her body held no secrets from me—I knew that she was incapable of any kind of self-destructive act. Thirdly: "[. . .] no other way out?" Well, no. My accusers should return to the beginning of this story: "There was no other way out if I wanted our love to endure, by any means possible."

But I fully comprehend what is being insinuated.

For once in their lives they should think.

If my real death had been a better solution, I wouldn't have hesitated. I would have thrown myself into the deepest of rivers (even though I hate water). But that wouldn't work. My simulated death presented Anita with all the advantages of a real death, plus one extra possibility: that of one day seeing me reappear, ready for a new love story. A possibility that only I could imagine? A possibility that absolutely did not cross her mind? I wouldn't have sworn to it. Swearing would have given short shrift to the mysterious waves that reverberate throughout the universe—for I could not imagine that, under the control of these mysterious waves, the molecules that made up my Anita (and which, therefore, held no secrets from me) would act in the same manner whether I were dead or alive.

These are my answers.

The most dismal of these options was the only one that allowed me to preserve a glimmer of hope.

SEVEN DAYS

One morning we reached such a high level of tension and exhaustion that we agreed not to speak to one another for an entire week, seven days.

THE CRIME

Seven days later, to the minute, Yves Somme, having arrived from Madrid, telephoned Anita and informed her that I was dead and buried. While he told her the story that we had very carefully imagined so that he could answer any and all of her questions, I took refuge in the studio, crying and wringing my hands.

Yves flew home to Madrid that same evening.

But three days later (I had hardly had the time to complete my dazed apprenticeship as one of the living dead), three days later, a Saturday, he had to return. A bolt from the blue: Anita wanted to pay her respects at my grave that Sunday.

Alecta was on tour. So Anita had telephoned "Simone" in Madrid and asked him to accompany her. Alone, she wouldn't have the courage.

Why? Why did she force this hardship on herself? Because she had doubts? Because doubt, the result of a long and winding path through one's network of cerebral convolutions, occasionally mars the delicate veneer of a clear conscience? Did she wish to confirm, like a police investigator, that I was truly dead? I couldn't help but wonder. Then I became ashamed of my own doubts. I was choked with tears. Anita wanted to pay her respects because she was racked by the greatest pain of her life, because, her heart broken, she longed to be at my side!

Whatever the reason, we had to act.

All hands on deck! We easily visualized what actions and ruses were necessary so that Yves and I could find ourselves at the tiny Mont-Cenis Cemetery, in the 18th arrondissement, in the middle of Saturday night attaching to a tombstone a marble plaque that gave my name, the dates of my birth and death and even, in the upper right-hand corner of the stela, a medallion with my likeness.

Yves returned from the train station where he had taken Anita after their visit to the cemetery. He didn't hide the fact that her mental state frightened him. She didn't speak. She didn't even respond when he spoke to her directly. She cried, in brief sobs or continual, silent tears.

Yves's every word pierced my heart like an arrow. (But, cruel fate, the final arrow reaches us only after death!)

We returned to the Mont-Cenis Cemetery to remove the plaque, put the old one back, and erase any trace of our crime. Then, back at rue Dodelat, we waited around until Yves had to go.

Had Anita been completely fooled? The question resurfaced in my mind several times, even though I mentally stamped my foot to ward it off.

I never knew that one could have such a lump in one's throat.

Yves left.

Alas, I would never see him again.

IN PRISON

Left alone, I thought I was dead (even though every single second I endured the torture of being on the brink of not dying), and until I received Yves's letter several days later, I unconsciously conformed to my state of death. I no longer went out, no longer ate, barely slept, or did so almost incessantly, I don't know.

I remember Sylvie Daumal phoned the night before Yves Somme's letter reached me. I remember having told her the rest of the story: the episode in the cemetery.

I remember having contemplated phoning Anita. A sword then sliced through my chest, and I fell into a long nightmare: it was a stormy night, I was alone, I was running, I was avoiding asteroids while stumbling over loadstars.

The apartment became my prison. The prison then continued to shrink and my body became my prison, then, as my deadly imprisonment wore me down even further, completely wore me down, the word *prison* itself became my prison. I fused with *prison* through a dimidiation and assimilation of my moribund being whose babblings managed to flow from my mouth in spite of my unconscious and immobile state. They commenced to re-count, as the flood of memories from a dying man recalls his past so that he might still believe in existence, the tale of what I henceforth was, *prison*. I told myself the story of the word *prison,* confusing myself with the sounds formed by the transmutations that the speech organs performed over the course of many centuries on the air emitted from my lungs, by the exhalation passing from my lungs through the windpipe and molded, before reaching the open air, by my vocal cords, my palate, my tongue, my teeth, my lips!

The vocal tract through which the air passes can open or close in varying degrees. The reader, if he wishes to better understand the story of my life, should pronounce the phoneme *a*: the opening is as wide as possible. If he pronounces, on the other hand, the sound *p* the tract closes completely for a moment. However, while the pronunciation of *p* and *t* require this complete closure, one does not confuse them; the difference arises from the fact that the occlusion does not occur in the same part of the oral cavity.

So these were the two material elements, the degree of aperture and the region of the oral cavity where the occlusion takes place—without forgetting the mimetic mental action itself (a sign that my mind had not ceased pulsating)—that determined my story from its start up to today (today!) in the form of the story of *prison*—and here's that story, in so far as I was capable, in my living dead state, of experiencing and witnessing it, of reconstructing it as if outside of my own self, pouring over a thousand manuscripts in the most infinitely vast library on Earth.

V

PRIZÕ

AT THE SAME TIME THAT NOBLE SPARTACUS WAS
BREAKING THE BONDS OF SLAVERY . . .

I saw myself leaning over the future *prison* in the middle of
his cradle woven from sound waves, when he first babbled
prĕhĕnsiónem.

In this series of phonemes, the vowel *ó* was accented with a
musical intonation: its pitch was higher than that of the other
vowels. And it was a long vowel, *ō*, whose utterance was more
elongated than that of the briefer *ĕ*.

Prĕhĕnsiónem soon started to change. The final *m* was hardly
audible—one now heard *prĕhĕnsióne.* The *h* sound, which was
initially analogous to the sound one makes from the rear palate when one is exhausted, or when one sleeps with one's mouth
agape, or when dying, was first reduced to a laryngeal breath,
produced by air passing over the edge of the vocal chords, and

then disappeared: *prĕĕnsióne*. This left the two *ĕ*'s in an uncomfortable hiatus, which was then resolved by the fusion of the two similar vowels *ĕĕ* in to a single one, *ĕ*: *prĕnsióne*.

Now on the other hand, the disappearance of the *n*, no longer pronounced before the voiceless fricative *s*, which was very slowly stealing its sonorous existence, led to a compensatory lengthening of *ĕ* into *ē*.

Already *prĕhĕnsiónem* was no longer *prĕhĕnsiónem*, but rather *prēsióne*.

IMPERIAL REIGN

Then the imperial reign commenced.

Over this period, three events affected the maturation of *prēsióne*.

First, its musical accent became a stress accent. Not that it had been exclusively musical beforehand and was exclusively expiratory afterward, but the accented syllable tended to be pronounced more forcefully than at a higher pitch.

Secondly, the contiguity between *i* and *ō* produced a hiatus. The tongue, in an attempt to put forth the least effort, pushed against the palate in order to bring its place of articulation closer to that of the *ō*, and then modulated into an approximant, *j*. This *j,* which is frequently called *yodh* after the tenth letter of the ancient Phoenician alphabet, together with *ō* formed the sound *jō*. (As for the *s*, "palatalized" by this *yodh* and thus drawn closer to the place of articulation on the palate, it became for this reason the palatal consonant *sj*.)

Thirdly, the vowels slowly stopped being either drawn out or short and instead differentiated themselves based on their timbre alone. The long vowels became close vowels; the short vowels became open vowels: ō et ĕ became ọ et ẹ.

Prēsiṓne was henceforth *prẹsjọ́ne.*

FALL OF THE EMPIRE

At the fall of the Empire, in the fifth century, the unity of the Romans' many territories crumbled. Hordes of barbarians invaded and wrecked havoc upon the provinces, quite unconcerned with maintaining the educational system and the proper functioning of its schools. These many events truly disrupted the development of *prẹsjọ́ne.*

During this troublesome time, the initial *ẹ*, after a series of modifications unique to the nature of *ẹ*, but also provoked by its proximity to that infamous *yodh*, should have changed into *wa* (*ẹj, ẹ́i, ẹ́i, ọ́i, ọ́ẹ, ọ́ẹ, ọ́ẹ, ọẹ́, uẹ́, wẹ́, wa*)—with *prĕhĕnsiṓnem* ending its days as *proison*, just as *mĕssiṓnem* eventually became the beautiful French word for harvest, "*moisson.*"

But it did not.

Plot twist: the *ẹ* closed, turning into *i*. This occurred under the influence of the past participle "*pris*" of the verb "*prendre,*" "to take," which was itself the progeny of *prḗso*, the form "*pris*" itself influenced by the preterite *prīsī̄*, child of *prḗsi* in which the *ẹ* closed due to the influence of the final *i*. And, analogously, *prẹsjọ́ne* became *prisjọ́ne.*

In this way, the mysterious mimetic force of the analogy reflected the meaning of the word. It did not therefore manifest itself with the same blind inevitability as the laws of sound, which could not see any farther than the acoustic imprint of the word they unrelentingly followed.

Prisjǫne.

SSSSSS, ZZZZZZ

In the word *prisjǫne* the consonant *s* was voiceless because the vocal chords don't vibrate during its enunciation, so it produced a sound similar to that of air under pressure from a small nozzle (*sssss*). On the other hand, if the vocal chords had vibrated, one would have heard a more musical sound and would have been dealing with its voiced congener, *z* (*zzzzz*).

Now the vocal chords, which were vibrating for the articulation of the two vowels *i* and *ǫ*, were forced to stop in order to articulate the *s*. A certain confusion followed in the coordination of these movements, which the larynx remedied in the most radical and lazy manner possible, by continuously vibrating, therefore voicing the *s* to become *z*: *prizjǫne.*

CLOSER TO ZJ

Between the articulation of the *i* and that of the *zj* enough time passed that a little transitory *yodh* sneaked in. This *yodh* was intended to facilitate the transition from one sound to the next by palatalizing the *i*—through a movement that brought the blade of the tongue towards the hard palate—palatalizing it by moving its place of articulation closer to the alveolar ridge, closer to *zj: prijzjǫ́ne*.

At this juncture the palatalized *zj* depalatalized. The *z* no longer felt the need to stick around on the palate next to the *yodh*, even though it had helped him take on the *ǫ*, and so decided to get rid of this now bothersome accomplice.

Seemingly swept up by this depalatalization, the articulation of the first syllable's *j*, which closely resembled *i*, melded with it: *prizǫ́ne*.

ONE QUESTION

Why did our speech organs undergo such contortions in an effort to facilitate pronunciation only to undergo the exact opposite in order facilitate the same task? Why would two dissimilar phonemes, merely because they were either contiguous or somewhat near one another, do everything in their power to become identical, whereas two similar phonemes that were near one another would move heaven and Earth to differentiate themselves?

Because a phoneme, meeting itself over the course of its lifetime, gripped with fear, death looming, during the decisive battle for its life, either melts back into itself or separates from itself with its final gasps and tries by whatever means possible to make itself seem different from its twin?

Because a word sometimes feels the need to tuck back in a limb that it had just stretched out five minutes before, for the sake of comfort and its general welfare, and is prepared to stretch it back out five minutes later for the same reason?

Prijzjǫ́ne became *prizǫ́ne*? Yes. Some sort of articulatory unity had been gained by *prijzjǫ́ne*, but only after great muscular efforts (of the tongue), which *prizǫ́ne*, all things considered, abandoned, preferring more clearly delineated sounds, which were more individualistic, and which therefore, in their own way, were easier to pronounce.

Prizǫ́ne.

WHAT HAD HAPPENED?

In the middle of the sixth century there was a new plot twist: the articulation of *ǫ* changed in timbre to become the diphthong *ǫu* (*o-ou*). Why? What had happened? Well, the close *o, ǫ*, had decided to close further in order to better affirm its identity and its personality in relationship to its brother, the open *o, ǫ*. The metamorphosis occurred in two steps: *ǫ* first doubled, becoming *ǫǫ*, then the second part of the vowel, as if it were frightened by this similarity, closed, becoming *u* (*ou*).

Prizǫ́ne had changed into *prizǫ́une* (*prizo-oune*)

THE FINAL *e*'S SILENCE

We have left the fate of the final *e* unsaid. This expression, alas, is only too fitting. Given its position as an outsider, this poor *e*, neither *ę*, nor *ǫ*, occasionally called mute (*ę̥*), never hurt sensitive ears with piercing tones: forever the last breath, it breathed its last at the end of the seventh century.

Prizǫ́un.

Prizǫ́un survived many a century without a single phoneme moving.

In the twelfth century, weary of such monotony, the speech organs decided to put their money where their mouth is, so to speak, (a reflex: just as one shakes a stiff limb) and get to work weaving a complex plot around *ǫ́u* and *n*.

To pronounce the vowel *ǫ́u*, one had to raise the velum from the palate, which then closed the nasal pharynx, preventing air from entering the nose. Conversely, the articulation of the nasal phoneme *n* required that the velum lower so that air could flow through the nose and mouth. But, due to chance, convenience, or laziness—following a confusion in the successive execution of contradictory articulatory movements (a confusion parallel to that which led to the voicing of *s*)—and then for those mysterious reasons which can lead a phoneme to assimilate or dissimilate itself—the velum was lowered prematurely when pronouncing *ǫu*, becoming nasalized in turn (which the Spanish tilde placed above it indicates): *prizõ̧un* (*prizon-oune*).

Since air from the lungs flowed through both the mouth and the nose when the nasal vowel *õ̧u* was being articulated, less air entered the mouth than for the articulation of the simple oral vowel *ǫu*. The air pressure on the mouth's muscles was consequently less forceful. The oral cavity tended then to open, and $\tilde{o}\tilde{u}$ widened to become $\tilde{o}\tilde{o}$, which quickly simplified into $\tilde{o}$: *prizōn* (*prizon-ne*).

1 2 , 1 3 , 1 4 , 1 5 , 1 6

Centuries marched on—12, 13, 14, 15, 16.

During the seventeenth century, the mouth organs, which had feasted on a general nasalization of the language in the twelfth century, suddenly found it unbearable that two nasal phonemes, $\tilde{o}$ and *n*, would immediately follow one another. Overcome with a need for dissimilation, they excised the final nasal occlusive, the *n*.

It was over. Other centuries passed.

Prizō.

"Prison."

Prison.

VI

MISTRESS ANNE
(The History of The Art of Medallion Making)

THE FIRST DAY

Ensconced in my humble abode for what seemed an eternity, I was still so weak that I could only crawl out. The regulars on the street themselves seemed not to notice me.

With a thousand precautions, I stood up.

Already, an unusually large crowd was pushing towards the heart of the city, and already the memories were flooding back. I recalled the time when we fought the invaders—our first cries breaking out from the processions, the shock of our contentious meetings, the fatal necessity of speaking the enemy's treacherous language and choosing someone among us to be King so that he could rule over us, our final defeat at their hands, the shame that the Chosen One was forced to follow the victor's orders and the sorrow that he had to impose them on us—and the time, even longer ago, of our glorious and silent communion.

The crowd pulled me along in spite of myself.

Yet, although my physical and moral energies were at their nadir, I wasn't distressed, for I was able to overhear the latest gossip, which elucidated stories that I had heard earlier, but had only partially understood.

A coup d'état was being planned in the shadows—a plot made all the more horrendous by the fact that this usurpative desire originated from the King's own brother, a duplicitous man, the second husband of a rich enemy princess, who had realized how to make the most of our enslavement.

This is why the perimeter of the Royal Palace was so heavily guarded. Only those closest to the sovereign were granted access. Among them was Mistress Anne. But the King wanted the people to have the opportunity to enjoy this great artist's medallions: starting in the morning, under the shade of a vast tent set up in the city's main marketplace, the works were exhibited, and it was there that our louring steps were carrying us. The King's decision stemmed from his concern to appease his subjects during a difficult time, but also, I was convinced, from a secret longing for the equality we had stripped from him one day long ago.

In the market square reigned a peaceful silence even though the entire citizenry seemed to be assembled there.

Men, women, and children filed through the tent under the vigilant eyes of the royal guard.

I awaited my turn.

The art of the medallion dated from the time of our servitude. It enjoyed great prestige among us, and we respected the many artisans who practiced it, but when it was a question of Mistress Anne, who was undoubtedly superior to all others, devotion was the best term. Born of one of our oldest families, she reached the peak of her glory when the King drew up a jealous contract with her granting him exclusive rights to the fruits of her labor. In exchange, she received great honors and privileges. Our exaltation then gave way to discontent: had we been so foolish as to celebrate an act that deprived us of one of the greatest joys of our lives? Moreover, it was whispered that Mistress Anne was sinking into a deeper and deeper depression every day. And the King himself, could he swear that a shadow of regret never tarnished his selfish pleasure? Finally today, even though the circumstances were unfortunate, but precisely in order to confront them as the salutary effect borne of the medallions' stark display unquestionably delivered us from our complacency, we had all gathered.

With indescribable emotion, I lost myself in the contemplation of the terracotta ovals, admiring the simplicity of their subjects—a melancholy portrait, a flock of animals grazing in a luminous field, a stormy sky—and the meticulousness of reproduction in such a small space.

I exchanged a few words with a soldier. If the King had taken so many precautions, he told me, it was for fear that the cursed brother, under enemy control, might become angry and order an attack to destroy the medallions. I chided myself for my misgivings: no, the King had not forgotten!

I was shaking from fatigue and hunger as I left the tent. Merchants' stalls were set up along the tiny streets adjoining the square. Having procured and voraciously consumed various foodstuffs, in spite of my fear that the sun might have spoiled them, I returned to my humble abode and immediately fell onto the heap of dead leaves that served as my bed.

My head buzzed with possibilities. I awoke relieved. So many memories lightened my heart, so many bold projects!

But a slight discomfort plagued my abdomen: had the previous night's food inflamed the seat of digestion?

I opened my door.

Just as many townspeople were heading towards the market square as yesterday. I joined them, and we walked in short, compact steps to pay our respects to the medallions.

My intestinal pain went away. Nevertheless, I preferred to abstain from eating. During the afternoon, I walked through the streets, observing the humble townsfolk. The profound silence, the scowling faces, the excessive zeal displayed in the completion of everyday tasks despite the heat, yet whose effort remained uncoordinated—perhaps the result of unrewarding work, as if they exhibited through these tasks an energy that they secretly reserved for other activities, led me to believe that some great revolution could break out if some propitious event were to transpire.

When I thought about returning home, my absent-minded wandering had led me farther astray than I would have wished. Suddenly fatigue and hunger plagued me.

From time immemorial, had Anita not told me of her fear that all food might be a source of death? (Anita, so solemn but jocose! When she wasn't enjoying the music we were listening to—*id est, exaggeranter, quando non audiebat nec J.-S.B. nec A.B. nec F.M.-B.*—she would turn to me and make pained expressions, then she would burst out laughing. Overcome with laughter myself, I would change the music according to her wishes.) But such reasoning, not eating to not die, biteth the taile, doubtfull, fallacious & uncertaine it be. If I wished to accomplish the project I had been crafting & have it goe from my braine, that is devoting myselfe to the art of medallion making, I must doe my dutie & fortifie & rowse my animall spirits, and so engorge all that I find, debarring poisonous mushrooms, with no worries, not even that a too-stuft bellie doth leaden the hand that would paint the terracotta: it seemes unto me that a man whose Stomacke is replete with various Cheer, & in a manner surfeited with drinking, is hardly able to conceive aright of Spirituall things; yet am not I of th'Opinion of those who, after long & pertinacious Fastings, think by such means to enter more profoundly into the speculation of Celestial Mysteries, & will I tell ye that the Writings of abstinent, abstemious, & long-fasting *Hermits* were everie whit as saltlesse, dry, jejune, & insipid, as were *their* bodies when they did compose them. 'Tis a most difficult thing for the Spirits to be in a goode plight, serene, & lively when there is nothing in the Body but a kind of Voidness & Inanitie, for withe the grievous pangs of Hunger the Stomacke begins to gnaw, & bark as it were, the Eyes to look dim, & the Veins, by greedily sucking some reflection to themselves from the proper substance of all the Members of a Fleshie Consistence, violently pulle down & draw backe that vagrant, roaming Spirit, careless & neglecting of his Nurse and naturall Hoste, which is the Bodie. As when a Hawk upon the Fist, willing to take her Flight by soaring aloft in the open spacious Air, is on a sudden drawn backe by a Lease tied to her Feet.

I then filled my emptie bellie with a thousand different items on the way home, and, once there, fell into a deep dreamless sleep.

VOCATION

The following day, having procured the necessary equipment, and pride and impatience prohibiting me from consulting a master artist whose orders I would have obeyed, I went to work: I wanted, by my own hand, to surpass all of them, even Mistress Anne! Such a desire elicited some feeling of shame on my part of course, if I thought about our former equality, but it was henceforth written in my heart. To ignore its call, which rang so loudly, would have left me lower than low, irrelevant and useless—and the mysterious hope persuaded me to think that, when all was said and done, the realization of this desire would be salutary, not only for me but also for my people.

Daily visits to view the medallions at the marketplace were my only apprenticeship. But I gazed at them in a new light: endeavoring to divine the techniques that had resulted in the solidity of a line or a burst of color, I found myself more inclined to see the evidence of the hand that made them than to unquestioningly accept the feeling of supreme joy they engendered.

The days passed, and my sluggish progress made them all seem the same.

One afternoon, my path crossed Mistress Anne's. She was as beautiful as the chroniclers had proclaimed her to be. Few townspeople knew her. She led an incredibly secluded life, only venturing out to visit the King, surrounded by many servants, her latest work held tightly to her chest.

So strongly did my devotion resonate that I dared to wave at her—and so incomprehensible is the fate of the world that she responded in kind.

From that day forward my work improved.

Save my visits to view the medallions, I no longer left my lodgings, which now functioned as a studio. Admittedly, my inexperience still all too frequently got the better of my inspiration and obstinance, and I would become irritated with a color that had dried too quickly, an inappropriate brush, or my skittish brushstrokes, which would make me paint outside the lines—or which, when too forceful, would spray my face with a thousand specks of color, so that at twilight some days, an observer might have believed I had spent hours comically making myself up, so hidden was my skin under a fanciful layer of colors, whereas one would have hardly even noticed the crude trifle that darkened the little terracotta oval on my easel.

Nevertheless, after some time I succeeded one day in painting a medallion, a young, nude virgin, that rivaled the works of the best craftsmen. I mused over this success for a long while, and managed over shorter and shorter intervals to repeat it, until the young virgin reached the highest point of beauty.

ANNE

One morning, dressed in a richly colored new outfit and clutching the medallion with virgin tightly against my chest, I set off for Mistress Anne's.

I knocked on the door of her magnificent and immense residence.

The head servant opened the door. He was a very tall, barbaric-looking man. Irritation reddening his face in reaction to my stammered question, I feared that his fists striking my head one after the other and driving me chest-deep into the ground would severely limit the possibility of Mistress Anne viewing the medallion. It took a great deal of time and cajoling to convince him to go and speak with the lady of the house. Upon his return: the medallion should be entrusted to him, he said, he would give it to Mistress Anne, and . . . No, I firmly told him, no.

A gladiator of his stature could have butchered twenty-four puny craftsmen such as myself with a frown and a shout, but— ready to run as fast as my legs would carry me—I told him no. I would be happy to describe the work in detail and he could relate every word of my description to the lady of the house, but no one but she could see or touch the medallion.

After hearing me out, he left, jaw clenched and eyes blazing with anger.

To my surprise, this second attempt met with success. The head servant, more conciliatory, requested that I follow him into the hallowed inner sanctum. We disappeared into long hallways, climbed and descended stairways, crossed rooms and interior courtyards, finally arriving in front of the area of the house where, far from the madding crowd, Anne practiced her art.

Standing in her studio, her long black hair falling about her shoulders, she recognized me: she had seen me, she said, one day near the market and had not forgotten me—she who, I thought proudly, unmoved by anything that was not terracotta, paint, or brushes had never, according to the chroniclers, noticed any man!

She then insisted we play a childish game: she wanted me to place my medallion on her work table. I must then turn my back while she placed her latest work next to mine. And only then could I look.

I understood why my description, which had been previously related by the head servant, had enchanted Mistress Anne: for, magically and unbelievably, I found that our two medallions were perfectly identical, as if the right eye and left eye each individually perceived the same virgin reproduced in her innocent nudity—to the point that, laughing and pretending to switch them, we were quickly unable to say who had painted which one!

Making love seemed the only appropriate action to celebrate this propitious moment.

The following morning, leaving my meager dwelling forever, I came to live with Mistress Anne.

Once a subject was chosen we would spend several days working on a series of sketches.

At times, we would rush in tandem to the bed that had been placed in the middle of the studio expressly so that we could act immediately upon our ardurous impulses. At other times, taken by a sudden wish for solitude, one of us would take refuge in a courtyard where the babbling of a fountain would calm our spirits—then soon irritate them, inciting us to return to the tyrannical sketch requiring our attention.

We never left the vast residence.

I feared the commentary of future chroniclers. Some would say that I wanted not only to plunder Mistress Anne's secrets, but also to distract her, to disturb her, to divert her attention away from her work so that my own egotistical plan—to launch myself above her and into the highest position—would be an even greater success, while others who were less jaded, understanding that my actions wielded a double-edged sword and that I had not escaped injury, would say that distracted as I myself was by my determination to distract her, I was silent for as long as she and didn't produce any further medallions—whereas yet others would say that all of this was nothing but pure fantasy on my part, that due to arrogance, I selected, exaggerated, and connected minute events in order to intertwine my own personal story with the history of the world: after all of their patient research, they might perhaps consent to imagine that a craftsman had lived at that time and place, and that one day, weary of the mediocrity of his own circumstances and work, he had decided to establish himself in the most promising studio of the most accomplished artist (a man, a woman, who could say?), and that was all—which would lead the most incredulous among them to believe, in the end, that the entire experience had never even taken place.

Those people made me burst with laughter—through an incomprehensible reflex, just as tickling elicits laughter—a laugh as powerful as a thunderstorm, a laugh that still splits my sides today (today!), a laugh so violent it would drive the silence from every nook and cranny of the manse and make the head servant come rushing back, even if he had just left us the moment before after having served one of those delicious meals that had been specially prepared for us, and whose careful preparation he himself oversaw in the sweltering kitchen.

THE PROMISE

The threat of usurpation was growing.

Sensing the futility of resisting the coup d'état whose inevitability was no longer in doubt, the king had secretly ordered the hurried construction of a palace on the other side of the mountains and was preparing to flee there.

He sent his most trusted messenger to Mistress Anne.

He had been shocked by her silence: had she given up her art, since she no longer presented him medallions with the usual regularity? Secondly, he encouraged her to join the Queen and him in their new palace. Indeed, as Anne was close to the monarch, she feared the worst for herself when the battle between the brothers eventually did break out, in spite of the number and valor of her servants.

Yes, Anne replied to the messenger (to whom she revealed her new life: her love for me, our regular, communal work, the perfect medallion we had imagined), yes, we would join them when the King so desired; he would not have been waiting patiently in vain, may this promise be relayed to the King! The messenger, a lanky but dignified man, told us the location of the new Royal Palace and the treacherous roads by which to reach it, and he left.

Soon, our preliminary sketches having removed enough un-
certainties that we believed the creation of the final medallion
would remove any that remained, we chose a pristine terracotta
oval, and, hearts pounding, drew the first lines as if we possessed
but one hand. From that moment forward, we didn't leave the
studio, concentrating all our energy on the perfect dance of our
brushstrokes.

And then the medallion was completed.

The union of our two bodies, which we indulged in without
further ado, truly sent us into the greatest raptures, yet Mistress
Anne and I both harbored a faint dissatisfaction, whose cause
we believed we could detect when we gazed upon the barely dry
artwork again. Yes, it was certainly the medallion we'd dreamed
of, but we found ourselves unable, we who had brought it to life,
to answer this question: what distinguished it from the other
medallion? The line wasn't steadier, nor the colors more correct, they weren't blended, nor did they flow more agreeably
than those of our virgin—yet a real and indefinable difference
that wouldn't reveal itself to our souls was definitely hiding
there—but would it reveal itself to the soul of the King, our liege,
that great connoisseur? Yes! Such was the well-reasoned conclusion we reached after a careful examination of various causes
and effects, questions and answers that seemed to parade past
our wild, staring eyes. Whether hope, pride, or folly, we imagined the King unearthing from this mystery the strength and the
vengeful force necessary to take back his kingdom and deliver
us from bondage, from the void—and, eventually, shrouded in

new-found glory, he would unite us, Anne and me, unite the most magnificent man and woman!

Anne slipped the medallion against her heart, between fabric and flesh.

THE HORSE

We departed amid the heat of darkening shadows. A clamor in the distance worried us. At the marketplace we discovered a dreadful sight: the tent displaying the medallions had been ransacked, the medallions were scattered on the ground, broken, the guards who'd been posted to protect them lay strangled!

A deserter was crossing the market square and I stopped him so he could tell us what had happened. The cursed brother, he explained, puppet of the colonizing enemy, yet filled by a sense of his own meager power, was massacring his own people. The violence and rapidity of the attacks had nipped in the bud any thoughts of resistance, as the King had foreseen. The enemy soldiers had laid siege to the city, and were committing acts designed to forever terrorize the citizens. They were forcing their unfortunate prisoners to recite oaths of loyalty to the new sovereign, the cursed brother, whose task, he himself proclaimed, would not be finished until he had killed his own brother, our King.

We needed to join the King at all costs.

Anne and I were no more perceptible than shadows as we crossed the town, following paths whose needless winding guaranteed our safety—and, finally, we left the city through an apparent dead end whose overgrown vegetation we cut through, granting us access to the vast countryside from which a mountain range rose on the horizon.

A congenial horse—which frightened us at first, its coat darker than the night from whence it came—approached. We mounted it and bolted off towards the mountainous horizon. Hindrances seemed not to exist to the animal, which kept up an even pace traversing both rocky and unstable lands, forests, rivers, and ravines as if we were crossing a flat, firm expanse, his hooves not even touching the ground.

We reached the mountains.

By dawn, we had descended the other side. The sunlight and crisp air reinvigorated us, and soon, thanks to the messenger's directions, which we had learned by heart, we found the new Palace. A small, paltry edifice, it was nestled sadly at the bottom of a chasm, but this placement was intended to better escape prying eyes.

The royal guard saluted Mistress Anne and led us through the hallways of the modest structure.

THE LETTER

The Queen, a gaunt woman of pale beauty, smiled at us. The King rose from his throne and greeted us, still majestic in spite of his reduced stature.

Anne placed the medallion in his open hand.

The King gazed upon it.

Alas!

The meaning, which escaped us, did not escape him!

A blissful expression came over his face, but suddenly . . .

How foolish we had been!

I blamed myself, in this chronicle I would one day recount with blind confidence, for not having stopped it at our moment of greatest hope, for the King, whose eyes widened suddenly, began to shake all over and recoiled, still staring at the medallion. He recoiled as if he had received a blow to his chest and fell so violently into his throne that the chair tipped backwards and hit the wall, causing a heavy halberd, which had been badly hung in the rush to prepare the palace, to fall, separating the Sovereign's head from his body in an incredibly bloody fashion.

A small division of enemy soldiers, who had explored the mountains under the traitorous brother's vigilant command, stormed the palace. Their savage shrieks melded with the mournful cries of the Queen.

Banishment was deemed the most severe punishment for Anne and the craftsman she loved.

We became lost in uninhabited lands, plodding, crawling, branches tearing our flesh, burned from the sun, alone, united yet divided by the horror of what had happened. We would walk, wandering for eternity, not only without any possibility of returning to the former kingdom, which would forevermore be the kingdom of death for us, but also, to an even greater degree, without persevering in the new one, which was not the kingdom of life!

Alone? But I could hear a noise. The noise of a small bell, the type of bell that farmers hang around the necks of livestock. But I didn't see any animals. I didn't see anything. I was alone.

Anita, alas, was not next to me in the bedroom.

The sound of the bell stopped and then started anew.

Someone was ringing the bell at the studio door downstairs.

The postman. An unstamped letter from Yves Somme, who, given the condition that he must have been in when he wrote it, had forgotten to affix a stamp to the envelope.

"When you receive this letter . . ." Those were his first words.

He begged my forgiveness.

VII

THE THIRD TALE
(excerpt)

AN OLD TESTAMENT

A thousand first sentences, if not to say all, rush to my quill with a howl of collective suicide.

For I had resolved to . . .

No, the truth is that I was incapable of making any resolutions: call Anita, not call her, model plaster, eat, sleep, go buy a musical instrument in an effort to decipher the notes in Miguel Padilla's red notebook, which, through pure lassitude, I had taken out of its drawer that very night . . .

However, through pure lassitude, without even really noticing, as a river flows, as a tree grows, I ended up recording in the notebook, in my clear and even script, after poor Padilla's illegible handwriting on the page where only the numeral III appeared, the first words of my story, but disguised, the first words of the story of a destitute man, barely surviving since time immemorial in a thousandth-class hotel of which he is the sole guest, until the day when, weary of the owner's (or manager's) harassment, and fearing death if he should stay, he prefers to confront his fears of dying should he depart, and departs down the street. An odd adventure, an odd love story destiny then held for him!

Then I would return Yves's now-full notebook to him in an effort to distract him from his perfect happiness.

PRIVATE DIARY, 1

Alas, the following morning I received a long letter from Yves. He had written first. He was speedier than I.

He related her murder and his death.

When I received the letter, he and Manuela no longer existed.

And he explained everything to me. Everything . . .

Yves, dead!

Once again, my life was shattered.

Yves, my Friend, my dearest Yves had bequeathed his apartment on the rue Manuel Dodelat to me.

I cried for an eternity.

Then I cloistered myself in the sitting room. There, I set aside my idea of a hotel from which the protagonist escapes—but I didn't close Padilla's notebook, because I then had the desire to relate the tale of real events (my departure from the hotel, Anita, my faked death, the notebook), something like a long letter to my Anita (165 pages), so that I could tell her everything and find solace in her presence in spite of my death . . .

... and in spite of Anita's—my angel's—death.

Would she read this letter one day? I both hoped and feared it.

I sat down in front of the red notebook and didn't move from the room on Passion's Way for countless hours.

The Diapason Adamentes IIIs singing softly in the background, (I had set the Audio Analogue 'R' integrated amplifier on one), I purely and simply wrote down my story, from the very beginning, as it had happened.

When I got to the present moment (it was nighttime), I set down my quill and went to bed.

The following morning, I took the train to L.—yes, to L.!—where I sold my apartment in Fourvière for much less than it was worth, especially since I had left all of my furniture. I had left everything; I took nothing (with the exception of four small metallic sculptures, which I had received from my deceased friend).

I went to L., to a realtor's office? Yes. To take care of business just like anyone else would have? My actions may surprise you, as they surprised me. But I never would have gone to L. if I hadn't received Yves's letter beforehand. Did this letter foment in me a vague revolt against destiny? Most certainly. Did Yves try to (and succeed in) transfusing a bit of his life to me through his words, in the way he had addressed them to me? Perhaps. Nonetheless, the death of my friend filled my veins with some sort of vital energy.

How was I to use this energy? To find Anita again. Selling the apartment? Only a pretext. But I knew that this reunion with Anita was impossible. Was it because I was dying for not having been able to make it happen? So? So, when you regain consciousness in the corner of a cell, in which, after having knocked you out, they threw you to rot without hope for the next thousand years, your first move is still to jiggle the knob of the door that's bolted from the outside with a thousand locks.

I did nothing else. Upon leaving the agency, I headed towards a telephone booth and I called—good heavens no! not Anita—but Alecta, in her small home in Cusset, an out-of-the-way neighborhood in Villeurbanne. I passed myself off as Anita's Italian cousin. (As it happens, she does have some family in northern Italy.) Traveling in France, I wished to catch up with my dear cousin whom I had met when she was living with Alecta, her friend.

Alecta waited three seconds before responding. Overcome by the gravity of what she had to tell the Italian cousin? Or because she had recognized my voice (in spite of my efforts to disguise it) and was getting ready to relate the lie that she and Anita had cooked up in case I were to come looking for her—which was exactly what I was doing? Which would imply that they had debated amongst themselves the possibility that I wasn't dead?

But wasn't that assuming too much? Yes—even though, as soon as it was a question of saving our love, I knew Anita capable of fighting tit for tat in this ruthless battle that brought us together—just as I had been capable of anything, and would be capable of much more, as we shall see anon, crossing the Rubicon of the imagination to save this love!

Alecta spoke, finally, murmuring in a barely audible whisper: "Anita is dead," she told me.

ANITA'S DEATH

Anita had drowned. She had fallen into the Rhone, under the Pont Wilson, several days before (May 28th). Two people had witnessed it from the bridge, but help had arrived too late.

It was not premeditated, according to Alecta. If it had been, she would have known, would have figured it out, one way or another, she was sure of that.

As for me, I was sure that Anita was incapable of such an act. I've said it before and I'll say it again: incapable of killing herself. I was absolutely sure. Absolutely? Suddenly, that was the rub! (When this sort of thing happens, you're no longer sure of anything.)

Absolutely sure. Sure that if I were indeed Anita's killer I would have gone and drowned myself right then and there!

But I couldn't believe in Anita's death. No more, I said to myself as I visited her grave, than she could have believed in mine.

GUILLOTIÈRE CEMETERY

Of course, there was this grave at the Guillotière Cemetery where I was paying my deepest respects . . .

When a break in my sobs allowed it, I gazed at the medallion affixed to the stela, which depicted the solemn yet sweet face of my beloved, and then the sobs would recommence.

Would Alecta and Anita come, as soon as I had turned my back, in order to unscrew the marble plaque and replace it with the correct one?

No, Anita was dead! The complexity of the hypotheses my mind had to conceive in order not to be convinced of this pushed me beyond the limits of human understanding. That Alecta and Anita could have . . . No, impossible. Absolutely impossible. Absolutely? That was the rub!

Anita was dead. Desecration of the sepulture, inquest at the police station, surveillance of her apartment, ruthless interrogation of Alecta—I could endeavor to make sure.

But I did nothing. She was dead.

But I didn't run off and throw myself in the nearby Rhone either.

I did nothing. Such was the nature of my love—and my madness—that I preferred to preserve the hope of seeing her alive again one day and to cultivate it with every passing second.

WHERE TO BE?

Upon returning to rue Dodelat, I foundered in the worst depression that I had ever known.

It was at this moment that fate resolved to use a new weapon to drive me even further into despair: with Anita dead, I found it intolerable to imprison myself in this apartment that had irremediably become my home, but which reminded me too much of both Anita's presence and absence.

I no longer knew where to be. Space was closing in on me, as if I weren't there. What to do, where to be—yes, where to be!—while waiting for the hope, which I previously mentioned, to become strong enough that I could once again endure living, dying, or agonizing in these rooms that were filled with her presence, here on Passion's Way?

The solution came from Sylvie Daumal.

I was ruminating on these questions when she phoned to find out how I was doing. She had recently called, the day before I received Yves's letter: I remembered that, in spite of the dense fog of confusion in which I was struggling at that time, and I remembered having told her everything.

Once again, I told her everything.

THE ACQUISITION OF AN AUTOMOBILE

The following day, I bought a car, I who had not had one in such a long time—and who so loved cars—so much so that I felt butterflies in my stomach when signing the enormous check. It was a fast and powerful Sublima S 24, an elegant machine I had always liked—a beautiful, bright red Sublima.

To hell with modeled plaster! I closed the door to my house, and with Padilla's notebook packed away in my luggage, I tore out onto the streets, death in my soul.

VIII

THE HEALER OF COUTY

COUTY

Annecy, in the Upper Savoy region of France, is not what one would call a large city. Rumilly, a nearby city, is most certainly a small one. As for Sales, a few kilometers from Couty, only a road sign indicates this village's existence. You don't notice anything special, just open countryside. Some noise in the distance, perhaps the bells from a herd of cows. Of course, if a townsperson informs you that it's very sparsely populated, if he offers to be your guide and to show you around, pointing out the town hall or the church right in front of your nose, you will eventually believe that Sales exists.

But then Couty, the hamlet of Couty! Nothing! One or two houses there? Maybe. If that lingering smoke isn't simply mist and fog. But perhaps if you climb that hill you might be able to make out some rooftops . . . ?

Nothing.

Nothing, except for one thing—but what an exception! What an exception, for it's in this locality, in this hamlet, in this backwater (I include this playful declension for Anita, to make her smile, just in case she might read these lines) known as Couty that Sylvie Daumal, after receiving her degrees in biology and medicine, and especially after the death of her parents, a very rich couple from Annecy who bequeathed their entire fortune to her, founded her laboratory.

In the heart of a glade (of a forest that she owned), she built a real little palace, a magnificent three-story home with turrets on each of the four corners (but the forest's large trees stood taller than the turrets, so one had to really emerge from the woods and into the glade in order to discover, astonished, the residence). The ground floor was only used as a garage and storage area. The living quarters were situated on the third floor, which included twelve rooms, filled with furniture and antiques from the thousands of houses that Sylvie's parents owned in France and throughout the world, and which she had sold after their deaths.

She lived in the right wing of the third floor.

The second floor was dedicated to the medical testing lab, famous in the region for the lady of the house's competence—as well as her kindness, charm, and beauty.

Couty was Couty Medical Laboratory. Couty was Sylvie Daumal.

CORNER ROOM

On June 6th, I moved into the immense corner room in the left wing of the third floor, which was sunny all day long (surprisingly, it was beautiful and even quite warm during my two-month sojourn in Couty). It was a room with a sculpted marble fireplace, a four-poster baldachin-style bed, a writing desk (on which the red notebook was placed that I filled with my neat handwriting every evening, page after page), armchairs, armoires, mirrors, paintings, sculptures, musical instruments—a violin, a spinet, a sixteenth-century vihuela in perfect condition, with its five, small, pierced rosettes arranged in staggered rows and six courses of double strings.

I hardly ever left the room, or as infrequently as possible. I lived almost like a cloistered monk.

RABBIT, 1

At the beginning of July, a farmer from Sales came to the lab one morning without an appointment just as it opened. His name was Marc M. Sylvie knew him well.

He was holding a wicker cage.

I was there when he walked into the lab. I was serving coffee to Sylvie and her two assistants, Y and Z. I had quickly remarked that neither of them seemed to like me very much, probably jealous that Sylvie adored me. And yet, I couldn't serve coffee to Sylvie and not to them.

SYLVIE'S LOVE

Adored: the word isn't too strong. Sylvie adored me—to the point, I'll say this straight off, of employing dishonest subterfuge in an attempt to pull me from the void into which she saw me sinking more deeply with each passing day, with each passing second. In an attempt to draw me closer to her, too? Undoubtedly. But there was no iniquitous malice on her part. I believe she did it unconsciously, almost as if she had a split personality.

I had a great deal of affection for Sylvie Daumal. But I felt neither love nor desire for her—all I had were love and desire for Anita, all I had was Anita's absence.

From our first days together, Sylvie managed to convince me that she was perfectly content with our arrangement. That my presence alone fulfilled her, that she wished for nothing else, that she was happy like this. I was naive enough to believe her. She was always in a good mood, unaffected, discreet. She respected my continual reclusiveness in my corner room. She didn't actively appear to seek my company. We saw one another infrequently, and never for very long—with the exception of a few evening conversations in a sitting room where the modeled plaster sculpture she had purchased from me on rue Dodelat occupied the place of honor.

She went out frequently to enjoy herself, as she had always done before my arrival: movies, theater, concerts, art exhibitions—typical outings. She would go alone, or with friends. In the past she had had many lovers, but since the start of our relationship, she unhesitatingly confided in me, she no longer had any. The fact that I lived under her roof fulfilled her. Such an attachment might seem excessive, but that's how it was.

Marc M., a somewhat uncouth individual, was carrying his rabbit in its cage to take it to the veterinarian's office. He believed it had contracted myxomatosis. But, having urinated before he left, he noticed that his own urine seemed abnormal, a bit dark. The lab was on his way to the vet's; he knew he wouldn't be putting Sylvie out (she was remarkably adept at putting people at ease), and so he had stopped.

He'd made the right decision, she told him. They would take care of him. However, morning urine that was a bit unusual should be no cause for alarm. Did he have a fever? No. And he wasn't alarmed either, but since he was driving right by the lab . . .

Intrigued by the rabbit, Sylvie wished to see it. The farmer opened the cage.

A wondrous baby bunny with a light gray coat and subtle auburn highlights appeared. It emerged from its wicker prison centimeter by centimeter, trembling all over with fear. It stopped, seeming to take in the world around him, and then suddenly scampered unhesitatingly in my direction. I bent down and picked it up. Its ears were pulled tightly against its head. Its entire body was shaking.

Its eyes were indeed slightly red. But it was shaking from fear, not fever. In my opinion, something had terrorized it, and its extreme fear had caused blood to rush to its head. The farmer had found it like this in his hutch, the door of which wasn't properly closed. Perhaps the rabbit had squeezed its way out and then became lost in the barn, where a horse had nearly crushed it under its hoof, unless a sheep hadn't acted as if it wanted to devour it. Still, it had been able to hastily return to its hutch and ensconce itself there, completely overcome with panic. Soon afterwards, incarceration in a wicker cage, a loud and bumpy journey . . .

I rubbed my cheek against its fur while speaking softly, and stroked its ears, which started to prick up again.

It began to calm down.

Blood started to flow more freely throughout its body. The redness in its eyes disappeared, as if by magic. Finally, it stopped trembling.

The farmer was a bit stubborn. I guessed it was hard for him to let go of his idea of myxomatosis. He wanted to know how his rabbit would act outside in the grass.

We all headed outside.

I set the rabbit on the ground in the clearing. It immediately acted normally: little hops, jumps to the left and right, searching for food, sudden, comical stops—it then sat upright on its bottom, front paws dangling, eyes staring, ears pricked, as immobile as a rabbit in a photograph.

Then, it suddenly started to gambol.

Sylvie was smiling, amused by the scene. Y and Z on the other hand looked sullen, almost reproachful.

"You'd say he was cured!" exclaimed the farmer, flabbergasted.

"He is cured," I said. (Crouching down to the rabbit:) "Right, my little bunny?"

The animal turned its head toward me, started to run, and jumped into my arms. Once snugly cradled in my left arm, it lifted his muzzle towards me, as if for a kiss, which I gladly gave it.

"You wouldn't be able to heal me, too?" Marc M. said to me, only half jokingly.

I had to hold back tears, the rabbit so reminded me of Anita and all her illnesses, which also resulted from her fears, and from which I had liberated her as well. But I also had a vague and mysterious impression, having given this rabbit a new lease on life, of having brought Anita and me closer together, of having eliminated a sliver of the death that had been separating us. To cure this man, and—believe it or not, I was already thinking about this—other people after him, wouldn't that be like reuniting with Anita little by little?

Sylvie asked the farmer about his urine that morning: a bit dark—but more reddish? More brownish? More greenish, it had seemed to Marc M., but you know how it is, you notice without really noticing, and then it's too late, you've flushed . . . No other symptoms besides, no specific illnesses at this time? No. Oh, yes, an ear infection, last week. He had taken some antibiotics. He felt fine now.

That's when Sylvie looked at me and fluttered her eyelashes, as if she had guessed my temptation to accept the man's offer and wished to encourage me, intimating that success, if I were to succeed, would be very beneficial to me.

But here's the trickery—here's what she was hiding from me: she knew of a new antibiotic used by ENT specialists, Tormicedel, which is taken in one dose, but which circulated through the blood for several days. The drug could occasionally lead to a slight greenish tinge in the patient's urine once or twice over the course of these few days, but this possibility was so rare that the doctor who had treated Marc M. for his ear infection hadn't thought it necessary to discuss it with him: this is what Sylvie assumed—

assuming as well, therefore, that the doctor had indeed prescribed Tormicedel and that Marc M. was one of these rare cases.

It was a bet, which she won.

The fluttering of her eyelids pushed me over the brink.

"I would definitely like to try," I said to the farmer. "With the authorization of . . ."

"Of course!" said Sylvie gently. "We'll check your urine afterwards."

Y and Z raised their eyebrows.

Sylvie ushered us into a small room. She recommended that Marc M. drink half a liter of water and then urinate in approximately one hour.

The man drank the water. I then asked him to lie down. I took his hand in mine. I assured him that he would be healed in an hour. He nodded his head. He was convinced. I felt that he had complete confidence in me.

Never releasing his hand, I didn't say another word, and concentrated on staring directly into his eyes.

Occasionally, he would drift off into a light sleep.

I admit without shame that I got into it and focused on his healing as if both Anita's and my salvation depended on it.

Victory! An hour later the farmer's pee was yellow like everyone else's. He notified the entire region that the biologist's new lover could heal both man and beast.

OUTLAW

Over the following days, I successfully treated several people who were suffering from more or less minor, and in most cases hypochondriacal, ailments, such as indigestion, insomnia, chronic itching, aches and pains, etc. Sylvie, of course, supervised all of my consultations.

Illegal practice of medicine? At times—how naive I was!—I worried for Sylvie. But she assured me there was nothing to fear. She was a doctor and well respected in the profession. In the eyes of the world I was her friend, her partner. I would sometimes speak to certain patients and offer them moral support, which they knew I willingly did, but I didn't accept any compensation, I didn't administer any potions—no, nothing to fear, the police weren't planning on surrounding the glade and taking the Couty Lab by storm.

Y and Z? No, she told me. Annoyed by my presence and my actions, absolutely. But they wouldn't cause any problems. They held their work with Sylvie too dearly, a position and an employer they knew to be irreplaceable.

I continued to treat, soothe, heal.

Was I on the right path or the wrong one? Still, it should be mentioned that Anita's absence was less dolorous when I slipped into my bed fit for a king at night, or rather that her presence within me was stronger and more real.

NIÉDASTAVIERNOSTSKAÏA

In mid-July I was presented with a more difficult case. Sylvie showed me the results of blood tests done on a woman who had leukemia, Tania Niédastaviernostskaïa. This woman was refusing the usual treatments. Her mind was made up. Her doctor had given up trying to convince her. The truth was that she was six weeks pregnant and her overriding fear was that the devastating chemical substances she needed to take might cause her to lose the baby.

People had so convincingly extolled my virtues to her that she was convinced she could defeat her illness if I helped her.

According to Sylvie, in whom she had confided, Tania Niédastaviernostskaïa wouldn't change her mind. No one could force her, and no one, medically speaking, could prove beforehand that she was wrong. She knew it. She had done her research. She knew that she wouldn't be the first to effectively combat leukemia in its early stages without the aid of conventional treatments.

Born in Russia in the farthest reaches of a Ciscaucasian valley, where people still believed in witches and all kinds of good and evil spirits, Tania was a seductive brunette, a little stout (though she had lost a great deal of weight by the time I met her). When she was very young she fell in love with a Frenchman from Chambery, a civil engineer on a humanitarian mission in her region, and left everything to follow him. She continued her studies in France. Intelligent and gifted, she became an art teacher at a school in Chambery. Then came the first tragedy in her life: her husband died in a car accident.

The years went by. She finally accepted the idea of starting a new relationship. She was nearing forty and wanted a child. But demanding and naive as she was, she also sought the ideal man. She believed she had found him—a painter ten years her junior. But this ideal man knavishly renounced all his promises as soon as he discovered she was pregnant.

The shock and sorrow had broken Tania. She started to lose weight. A doctor (a friend of Sylvie's) had recommended she have some blood tests done, just in case. As soon as she learned the results, she had decided to treat herself in her own way—desirous, above and beyond everything else, as Sylvie told me, not to lose the child.

DEATH LURKING

I decided to cure Tania Niédastaviernostskaïa in twelve days. Each day the disease would recede a bit more. We would then wait three days, she would have new blood tests done, and the leukemia would be gone.

A crazy certainty kept me going: if I succeeded in chasing away the death that was lurking around this woman, I would have made a vital step towards Anita.

Tania embarked on the adventure with absolute faith. She visited me in my corner room for half an hour every day for twelve days. During the half-hour session, I would hold her hands and look into her eyes, without speaking, or saying very little.

Nothing else.

She visited no doctors.

Her chronic fatigue steadily improved and by the eighth day she had stopped losing weight.

I took care of several other people during these twelve days. Since I had started my new occupation, my failure rate was zero. It's true that most of these people had nothing wrong with them. One might almost believe that only the healthy consulted me, or that disease no longer existed the world over.

THE TRUTH

Now, without further ado, I'll tell you the truth: Tania had nothing wrong with her either. Her fatigue and her weight loss were nothing but the result of despair eating away at her. And if, after a fortnight, her results had returned to normal, it's because they'd never ceased to be so. The first set of results Sylvie had shown me? Believe it or not she had falsified them (at least that's what she had to admit to me the evening of July 31st). Because she adored me so, in the hope that the joy of healing would put me on the path of healing myself, and in the hope that, perhaps, living under her roof and experiencing moments as inspiring as Tania's resurrection with her, I would start to love her. I have already noted these hypotheses concerning Sylvie's motivations.

THE SECOND HALF OF JULY

I continued to treat the populace's minor complaints (not everyone was a Niédastaviernostskaïa) while keeping Padilla's notebook up to date.

In spite of my refusal of any kind of remuneration or gift, Tania, who had noticed paper and pen on my writing desk and who revered me, offered me a magnificent gold pen.

I was coming back to life. Not that I resembled a convalescent, slowly recovering from some horrible disease: rather, I resembled a shadow that was flourishing and growing in a state that one might have thought excluded all flourishing and growth: that of the living dead. Buoyed by the certainty that I was on the right path to finding Anita, I was steadily progressing towards the nameless country that had always been my one and only true home—and whose border seemed, suddenly, to no longer recede with each step I took.

July 31st marked, it's true, a devastating setback.

As for the crushing revelation that had been afflicted upon me the night before, on July 30th at 10:00 P.M., it nearly put an end to the journey.

WITHIN THE PALACE WALLS

Despite my precautions and Sylvie's interdiction to anyone penetrating the walls of the manse where I practiced my art, a journalist from Annecy, W, took a photograph of me without my knowledge. He worked for a regional monthly magazine, *Eye on Annecy*, and my portrait accompanied by an article was to appear in the August issue, which I didn't know, but which I learned when . . .

Well, here it is.

On Saturday the 30th, as at the end of every month, Sylvie invited Y and Z to dinner at a luxurious inn in Rumilly. She was thus able to maintain an appearance of cordiality with her assistants, who, by the way, she didn't hate and who were good biologists.

Left alone, I ate quickly in the kitchen.

After dinner, I recorded the last part of the Niédastaviernost-skaïa incident in the red notebook: the gift of the golden pen.

At 9:30 P.M. I put my pen down (the beautiful pen from Tania).

At 10:00 P.M. I was lying in my immense bed—thinking of Anita—when I heard a car stop in the glade and a door slam shut.

I got up.

Someone who was suffering from some sort of attack and was coming to see the healer in the dead of night? Sylvie, coming home earlier than expected?

I looked out the window. I saw a car I didn't recognize.

I walked down the stairs.

Someone was ringing the doorbell.

I opened the door.

Alecta!

APPARITION FROM BEYOND THE GRAVE

An apparition from beyond the grave wouldn't have surprised me more. But it was definitely Alecta, living, blonde, attractive—even if I always found her pale and out of breath.

"Is Anita alive?" I immediately exclaimed.

I asked her if Anita were alive! Such were the first words I could utter, that I uttered in spite of myself, that came out all by themselves!

If she feigned astonishment, if her expression belonged to someone who thought I was clearly demented, it was because she was a great actress—she was a remarkable actress, destined for success, as long as her asthma allowed it.

I quickly added:

"Forgive me, Alecta! I beg of you, forgive me! I can't believe she's dead. I can't. Forgive me . . ."

"I understand," she said softly. "Nor can I. I can't believe it."

Did she understand why I was asking her forgiveness? Was this what she understood? I held my mind back from being pulled into the maelstrom that a question such as this bored through the very fabric of the universe.

"I'm not myself," I said to her. "And the shock of seeing you here . . . But you're out of breath! You don't feel too well, do you?"

"No."

"Come inside. I'll explain everything and ask for your forgiveness! Come in."

I had to help her up the stairs. Speaking with difficulty, she clarified the mystery of her presence in Couty.

She had followed Mikhail the mime's advice. Thanks to a recommendation letter from the renowned artist, a talent agency had booked a tour in the area: Aix-les-Bains, Annecy, and tonight, the last and most important stop, Chambery—yes, at this very moment while speaking to me, she should have been at the Chambery Municipal Theater—but an asthma attack had laid her up since this morning. She had cancelled the performance. Towards the end of the afternoon, she had nevertheless received a journalist from *Eye on Annecy*, a certain W, for an interview that would appear in the September issue. As he was departing he left her the August issue, which was yet to appear at newsstands. She had flicked through it, and . . .

So, I was alive! So, I had made Anita believe . . .

She had then decided to see me before she left. (She was returning to L. that same night.) When she phoned, she had only reached the answering machine with Sylvie's voice indicating when the lab was open.

She had stopped by.

It was now my turn to dispel the mysteries. I told my story to Alecta, from the first word to the last, my faked death, the telephone call from the Italian cousin, my exile in Couty, everything, leaving nothing out—save the doubts that I had had—and that I still had?—but she knew enough about that!—concerning the real death of Anita.

MY CHILD

When I had finished speaking, Alecta said nothing for several moments. I thought she was stunned by what she had just heard. But there was something else. I knew there was something else.

Alas!

"I'm hesitant to tell you something so dreadfully heartbreaking," she told me. "But I believe I must. Yes, I'm sure I must. Not long before Anita's death . . . You know she told me everything. I had been worried since what had happened . . . I feared for her health, nothing else. I didn't think it could be from . . ."

She stopped. She sobbed. I didn't understand. She seemed to be talking to herself. A kind of terror overtook me.

"Tell me, Alecta. Tell me!"

She gathered her strength to continue:

"I forced her to go to the doctor's office. I went with her. When Anita died . . ."

"Well?"

"She was pregnant."

I didn't kill myself before Alecta, I know that today (today!), because a plan immediately formed in my mind . . .

But this project wouldn't truly take shape until a little later, during my return trip.

I burst into tears. Alecta started to cry, too.

Being together became unbearable. Anita was too present between us. Alecta told me she was going to leave.

PENULTIMATE MIRACLE

I sat down beside her.

"You have such difficulty breathing!"

I took her hand and held it tightly. Nothing was said. We didn't speak of her illness, and the word "heal" wasn't uttered. But we both knew what I was attempting to do, with her consent.

I looked into her eyes. Never had I been so sure of myself: then came the moment when I knew her asthma would no longer plague her, that it would no longer prevent her from living, that it would no longer prohibit her from staging her mime performances for which she had such a gift.

And, at that moment, I decided to return to rue Dodelat. Alecta had been my last patient here. I would no longer be the Healer of Couty. I told Alecta and asked her to call me as soon as she liked to let me know how she was doing.

She left soon after.

I stretched out on my bed.

When Sylvie returned, I wanted to talk to her, to inform her immediately of my departure, but I found myself unable to move. Alecta's revelation had turned me into a block of physical and mental suffering, occasionally affected, it's true, by a strange glimmer which I couldn't yet recognize for what it was—you can search right up until the last second, death conceals itself well—a glimmer of hope.

IN SPITE OF EVERYTHING

The following morning, quivering from insomnia, I went to see Sylvie before she started work. Following our normal protocol, which had been established over the past several months, I told her everything, naively, with a naive sincerity. I spoke to her about Alecta's visit—and about what Alecta had told me.

And, embarrassed, I informed her of my decision to return home. But she helped me. She knew how to help me overcome this embarrassment: comprehension and kindness, and the right tone. She was still the Sylvie Daumal that I knew, that I thought I knew.

I announced that I would leave the following day, August 1st.

Until then, no more patients. The healer was gone, sick, dead, he could no longer heal; she could say whatever she felt was right, but I no longer wanted to see anyone.

Then I returned to my room.

SEXUAL ENCOUNTER, 2

During the afternoon, I fell asleep without realizing it. Then followed two hours of nightmares from which I awoke sweating, trembling and in tears.

I stayed in the shower for a long time. Then, too weary to dress, I lay back down on the bed in my robe.

A few minutes later Sylvie knocked on my door. She never came to my room. She walked in and sat down on the edge of the bed. Perhaps she thought I was ill. She put her hand on my forehead. I closed my eyes, from fatigue, from distress, from loneliness.

I didn't move when she began to caress my face and then my chest. I kept my eyes closed. I gave my body over to her, letting her open my robe, letting her touch me more, as much as she wanted, any way she wanted. Why? Out of pity, as she might have believed, pity mixed with egotistical pleasure? To offer alms through physical contact—which would show her, alas, in case the slightest doubt may have lingered in her mind, that she didn't arouse me at all (for I didn't say a single word, I didn't make a single movement, not even a simple reflex, even though her increasingly forceful caresses released from my body a thousand spurts of semen, which rose and swirled around the room like a whirlwind)?

No.

Why? I don't know. Because I was dead. It's because I was dead that my body was overcome by an orgasm but no feeling of pleasure reached my brain—and that I was incapable of the slightest word, the slightest movement—a single movement might have perhaps saved Sylvie Daumal, simply brushing my fingers against the back of her hand—but I was incapable, I was disappearing, I was burrowing deeper and deeper inside myself, I didn't even open my eyes, I didn't even hear her leave the room—and when I was finally able to look around, I was alone.

Sylvie always dressed well. When I saw her again that evening, she was wearing an elegant black dress and was getting ready to go to the Marquisats Cultural Center in Annecy to see the singer Marc Ogeret who was scheduled to sing songs of the Paris Commune.

I asked for her forgiveness.

She knew me better than anyone, I told her. She knew my mind was free of any ill-intentions towards her. She had to know that. Could she please forgive me. But then she asked my forgiveness. Forgiveness? For what? For being the best a woman can be? For having helped a poor soul, a moribund, a sculptor of the thousandth order who, what's more, no longer sculpted, a shadow of that sculptor? For having committed the grave sin of showing me too much love?

No, she told me, her face suddenly unrecognizable, disfigured by her distress, no, there was something else, a feeling of remorse that had haunted her for the past few hours . . .

It was then that she told me about Tormicedel, the drug that had indeed been prescribed to Marc M.—and especially about Tania Niédastaviernostskaïa's falsified lab results, an ignoble act of treachery, the thought of which troubled her deeply, no, she couldn't get over having deceived me, even through love! Furthermore, she was now suffering from having removed any illusion I might have had of my powers, thus destroying the only miniscule excuse for her crime! She herself had fallen into the trap, the damage was complete and irreversible.

I did everything I could to calm her down. (Remorse? But it was I who set her down this dark path, if she were to reflect on it . . . Anita . . . Klehr's Syndrome . . . !) I did everything I could to calm her down and I think I succeeded. Why? Because I was sincere. I didn't hold it against her that she had lied to me, or that she had told me the truth. But why? My indifference to these revelations disconcerted me. Why such indifference? I then understood that, since Alecta's visit, Sylvie no longer really existed for me. That her confessions didn't affect me any more than her caresses, that I had already left Couty, that Couty had already been wiped from the map!

Also, her story of rigged lab results by no means shook my faith in my healing powers.

Let me add, I know today (today!) that the execution of my ingenious plan required that I blindly believe in these powers. I couldn't have the slightest shadow of a doubt. It was as if she had said nothing to me—besides, had she told me the truth? And lost as she was in her adoration, did she herself even know if she was telling me the whole truth? Yes, it was as if she'd said nothing. There you have it!

FAREWELL

I accompanied her to her SUV parked in the clearing near my red Sublima S 24 in the shade of the tall trees. The weather was so pleasant, and had been for such a long time, that we never parked inside. We enjoyed walking across the clearing and sitting down in our cars, which had absorbed the gentle warmth and sweet smells of the forest. Y and Z themselves, narrow-minded and meticulous, but only because of their parsimoniousness, left their cars outside, even though the doors of the immense ground-floor garage were left wide open for them.

Sylvie and I were gradually recovering our composure. I smiled at her. She managed to smile back, her eyes still wet. We hugged warmly as dear friends, and she quickly climbed into her SUV.

She left down the narrow driveway, which, after a few meters, joined with a small road that was hardly any less narrow. As she merged onto this road she turned around and waved.

AN UNKNOWN DRIVER

Just before midnight, two police officers from Annecy arrived at the lab. A betrayal? Had Y and Z, less timorous than we had thought, played a dirty trick?

That was preposterous. Especially at midnight!

No. The police officers had come to inform me that Sylvie Daumal had had an accident between Annecy and Rumilly and that she hadn't survived her injuries. Had she misjudged a curve, had she tried to avoid an unknown driver to whose presence the police had already been alerted, a crazy man who went up and down the roads at night, indiscriminately driving on the left and the right? Nonetheless, at the end of a curve Sylvie had hit a tree at full speed.

She died while being transported to the hospital. Her last words requested that I be informed of the accident.

Once the officers had left, I cried for a long time. I cried for the dead—Marianne, Anita, Yves, Sylvie. I cried for my own death.

Then, I gathered my things.

I drove all night.

By morning I was back at rue Dodelat. I had continued to cry, to cry my eyes out. But a plan had formed in my mind during the return trip.

Forgive me, my dearest Anita, for the suffering we are yet to endure.

IX

DYING

SELF-PORTRAIT

All was silent on rue du Pasado Rey this first day of August.

I locked myself in the sitting room with a drawing Anita had made of herself using simple features and naive colors (one of the self-portraits she drew while phoning Alecta) and I kept my gaze fixed on my beloved's face for hours, perhaps days.

I set the drawing down next to me on the sofa and waited.

My plan was to resurrect Anita.

I had saved Tania Niédastaviernostskaïa from death. Life owed me a life. Life owed me Anita's life, without me needing to further sacrifice my own life for my beloved, a sacrifice that had resulted in her death!

As soon as I had arrived, I'd returned the red notebook to the lower drawer so that I would no longer take pen to paper (Tania's beautiful, gold pen, which I set next to the notebook), for I could feel nothing but anticipation. There was only space, both in my mind and my body, for a resurrection plan.

I had returned the red notebook to the lower drawer so that I would no longer take pen to paper.

How, under these conditions, was the end of my adventure, to the very last word, reproduced there, such is the mystery, such is the question to which no journey into other realms could ever provide an answer—and such is death, everything except death.

RESURRECTION

I waited.

My right hand placed on the drawing, at which I henceforth no longer gazed, I waited for hours, perhaps days, still cloistered in the sitting room on Passion's Way.

One night—at two in the morning—the phone rang.

It was Alecta.

Alecta!

"Cured?" I immediately asked her.

"Yes, cured!"

I took her answer as a good sign.

She only answered with this "yes"—then, very quickly, in a weak voice, her throat tight with unparalleled emotion, said:

"Anita is here, next to me! Living, beautiful, and whole. The Anita that we know! It's a miracle! She wants to talk to you . . ."

I must have lost consciousness for a moment, not long enough to drop the telephone—not long enough to die.

I then uttered the name of my beloved:

"Anita?"

"Yes!"

It was definitely Anita who had just pronounced that "yes," both intense and fragile, Anita and not Alecta, or anyone else; I couldn't let myself harbor any doubts!

"My dear! I'm coming, I'll be there! I'm on my way. I'll be there!"

"Yes!"

I was overcome with emotion. I couldn't say anything else.

"Ah!" she said.

My God! All of her fears and all of her love were combined in that lost child's "ah!"

"Yes, my angel, I'm here! Tell me!"

"You still love me the same?"

She often used to ask me that question, with those same words.

"Yes, my dear! And do you?"

"Me too, the same!"

I wanted to keep talking to her—I wanted to talk to her about the child—but suddenly I heard a crash, some confused noises, then Alecta's voice ("Anita!")—then nothing. Silence.

I screamed her name twice: Anita, my dear, Anita!

It was Alecta who answered in a calm voice:

"Don't worry, she'll come to. She's exhausted, but the blackouts don't last long. She'll come to. She's fine, I swear."

Her confidence, her certainty gave me strength. I had to leave, quickly. Alecta explained to me precisely how to find them once I was on rue Charles Robin.

"I'm on my way, Alecta! Tell her that as soon as she wakes up! Take care of her, do anything you have to, I'm counting on you! I'm on my way. Wait for me!"

HYPOTHESES

I jumped into the Sublima. My faithful car seemed to share my haste, shuddering all over, acting as if it were anxious to be in L. at this very moment.

I left the city.

Anita alive at Alecta's . . .

The devil (it could only have been the devil himself) endeavored to put the idea of some kind of conspiracy in my head, the idea of some horrible vengeance, of a trick set up by Anita and Alecta—but I knew how to thwart his craftiness.

Anita . . . Exhausted, my dear, my Anita! After such Herculean efforts . . . My God! How did she pull herself from the grave, and . . . No, no! If there was a miracle, why imagine such horrors? If there was a miracle, then she had never drowned and had never been buried! She had forgotten everything about death. She was alive, beautiful, and whole, her unborn child still alive inside her!

I REMEMBER HAVING SAID TO MYSELF

The kilometers flew by in no time at all. I don't know how the hours passed. I remember having said to myself, after the halfway point, that from this moment forward I was closer to rue Charles Robin, Alecta's street, than to my home on Pasado Rey—and then I arrived.

I drove through L. and Villeurbanne, which were both deserted, before entering Cusset, a kind of a large village inside the limits of Villeurbanne itself. (Yes, the events recounted here date from an era before the great demolition and reconstruction, which have given the area an homogenized look.)

FOLLOWING THE SAME PATTERN

It was then that a violent thunderstorm broke out, as they sometimes do in L. during the month of August.

Although I had memorized the route, I had great difficulty finding rue Charles Robin. I finally found it. It was off rue du 4 Août, almost a continuation of rue de Madrid. It was a narrow and not terribly long semicircular-shaped street, a vestige, it seemed, of a former housing development for factory workers, for the old-fashioned houses that bordered it all looked the same.

Hardly had I turned down the street than a series of gusts of unbelievable strength forced me to stop. Then a power outage plunged the entire neighborhood into darkness. I started moving again, searching for number 6. But I saw only rain, dense and white in my headlights, as if the whole city were underwater.

When a series of four or five successive lightning strikes allowed me to figure out where I was, I realized that I had driven past number 6, and that I was in fact at the end of the street. I drove around the block—Petite rue Pasteur, rue Bergonier—to head down rue Charles Robin from the beginning again.

Tremendously nervous and shaking uncontrollably, I decided to search on foot this time, walking along the row of houses. I abandoned the car and braved the raging elements.

Less than a minute later, soaked, blinded, covering myself up against the gusts, I was lost.

But number 6 couldn't be too much farther.

I walked up to the first house.

In spite of the claps of thunder and the torrent of rain, I heard a faint grating above me, like the sound of rubbing metal, faint but distinct, without paying too much attention to it.

But I heard it.

Suddenly the electricity came back on. The neighborhood was illuminated once again.

I raised my eyes.

Number 6!

WHAT WAS HAPPENING?

I followed Alecta's instructions to the letter: as I rang the bell, I opened the door on the ground floor, entered, and found myself in a kind of storage room with a staircase climbing along the left-hand wall. The staircase led to the living quarters on the second floor.

My foot hadn't even landed on the first step when the door at the top of the stairs opened.

Anita?

Or rather Alecta, who must have come running when I rang, who was going to take me to Anita—lying in bed, pale, weak, but smiling and holding me as tight as she could in her arms, in a surge of infinite joy . . .

But the person who appeared at the top of the steps was neither Alecta nor Anita.

It was a man with long, white hair wearing a light-colored suit. His eyes sparkled. Who was this man, and what was happening?

FINAL HYPOTHESIS

A simple explanation immediately came to mind: the houses on this street were dilapidated and falling apart. The rusty nail that held the number 9 upright must have given way under the wind's onslaught. The number must have then pivoted around the lower nail (the grating that I heard), and the 9 metamorphosed into a 6.

Believing that I had entered number 6, in reality I was inside number 9 rue Charles Robin.

At least that's what I assumed.

PANTOMIME

I was just about to speak, but the man—who didn't seem surprised to see me—mimed an imperative, questioning gesture towards me. Leaning on his right leg, his left leg only touched the floor with the tip of his toe, his head lifted, mouth agape, eyebrows raised, arms slightly spread away from his body, everything about him urgently asked me: "Yes, no?"

So pressing was this silent inquiry that I wanted to indicate to him, before uttering any words, that he was wrong, that I didn't know anything, that I was there by mistake—I therefore hastened to raise my hands while shaking my head from right to left in three or four quick movements.

But I wasn't answering no to his question, as the monster thought! I wasn't answering no to his question. I was denying the whole situation, him, the house, his wait, which didn't concern me, his apparent certitude that I knew, whereas I knew nothing and didn't want to know anything; I was saying no to everything!

But the man, wildly impatient, gleaned only one thing from my pantomime: "No!"

THE SCREAM

A fierce look flashed across his face, more deadly than the thunderstorm's lightning flashes.

Emboldened by this no, encouraged, determined by this no, he rushed back into the apartment at the very moment I was going to speak—and almost immediately I heard a scream of terrible suffering, extremely shrill, sustained, unending, a scream that paralyzed me and made me suffer as well—whatever the being who howled in this manner was enduring, the imagination couldn't fathom it.

An eternity of suffering was held in this scream.

The scream stopped.

I came back to life and regained the ability to move.

What to do?

But I didn't have the leisure of pondering that question: behind me, the front door opened. I turned around, ready to confront any unknown danger.

I thought I'd lost my mind—perhaps I did lose my mind.

For I saw a man enter, and this man was me—he looked exactly like me—and he was dressed the same way I was!—I saw the man of whom I spoke in the first lines of this story enter, this other me who was appearing here, now, almost at the same time as I had, at number 9 or some other address on rue Charles Robin!

But his hair and clothes were dry. Had the storm stopped? The sky I could make out through the open door had a strange hue, the hue of another sky.

I saw no other houses.

The man walked close by me. He stopped for an instant, barely—it wasn't really a complete stop—and we looked at one another, and I thought I was dying!—but everything happened so quickly, and so numerous and contradictory were the impulses that disturbed my mind and my body, that I was paralyzed—and I saw in his eyes that he had been horrified by the scream we had just heard, horrified by the unspeakable sorrow that my unintentional negative response had engendered—would he, relieved, have decisively nodded yes?—for there was nothing of the previous moments that escaped him, of that I was certain! He was horrified as well by another sorrow that this same response could engender and of which this time I would be the victim if I were to remain there: how else could one explain the quick but imperative movement of his head towards the door, a simple nod, but one which had the impact of an irrefutable order, like the visible expression of some sort of irresistible mental shove, and which I felt in my entire being!

Suddenly he stopped looking at me. He walked away and started up the stairs.

As for me, I headed toward the door, asking myself, my mind now free of all other thoughts, if I was destined to see Anita and if our child was destined to be born.

RENÉ BELLETTO was born in 1945. He is a screenwriter, guitar teacher, poet, and novelist. He is the author of numerous books of fiction, criticism, and poetry, including the novels *Eclipse* and *Machine*. His novel *L'Enfer* was awarded the Prix Fémina in 1986.

ALEXANDER HERTICH is an Associate Professor of French at Bradley University. In addition to translating, he has written about Jean-Philippe Toussaint, Raymond Queneau, and other modern French novelists.

PETROS ABATZOGLOU, *What Does Mrs. Freeman Want?*
MICHAL AJVAZ, *The Golden Age.*
The Other City.
PIERRE ALBERT-BIROT, *Grabinoulor.*
YUZ ALESHKOVSKY, *Kangaroo.*
FELIPE ALFAU, *Chromos.*
Locos.
IVAN ÂNGELO, *The Celebration.*
The Tower of Glass.
DAVID ANTIN, *Talking.*
ANTÓNIO LOBO ANTUNES, *Knowledge of Hell.*
ALAIN ARIAS-MISSON, *Theatre of Incest.*
IFTIKHAR ARIF AND WAQAS KHWAJA, EDS., *Modern Poetry of Pakistan.*
JOHN ASHBERY AND JAMES SCHUYLER, *A Nest of Ninnies.*
HEIMRAD BÄCKER, *transcript.*
DJUNA BARNES, *Ladies Almanack.*
Ryder.
JOHN BARTH, *LETTERS.*
Sabbatical.
DONALD BARTHELME, *The King.*
Paradise.
SVETISLAV BASARA, *Chinese Letter.*
RENÉ BELLETTO, *Dying.*
MARK BINELLI, *Sacco and Vanzetti Must Die!*
ANDREI BITOV, *Pushkin House.*
ANDREJ BLATNIK, *You Do Understand.*
LOUIS PAUL BOON, *Chapel Road.*
My Little War.
Summer in Termuren.
ROGER BOYLAN, *Killoyle.*
IGNÁCIO DE LOYOLA BRANDÃO, *Anonymous Celebrity.*
The Good-Bye Angel.
Teeth under the Sun.
Zero.
BONNIE BREMSER, *Troia: Mexican Memoirs.*
CHRISTINE BROOKE-ROSE, *Amalgamemnon.*
BRIGID BROPHY, *In Transit.*
MEREDITH BROSNAN, *Mr. Dynamite.*
GERALD L. BRUNS, *Modern Poetry and the Idea of Language.*
EVGENY BUNIMOVICH AND J. KATES, EDS., *Contemporary Russian Poetry: An Anthology.*
GABRIELLE BURTON, *Heartbreak Hotel.*
MICHEL BUTOR, *Degrees.*
Mobile.
Portrait of the Artist as a Young Ape.
G. CABRERA INFANTE, *Infante's Inferno.*
Three Trapped Tigers.
JULIETA CAMPOS, *The Fear of Losing Eurydice.*
ANNE CARSON, *Eros the Bittersweet.*
ORLY CASTEL-BLOOM, *Dolly City.*
CAMILO JOSÉ CELA, *Christ versus Arizona.*
The Family of Pascual Duarte.
The Hive.
LOUIS-FERDINAND CÉLINE, *Castle to Castle.*
Conversations with Professor Y.
London Bridge.

Normance.
North.
Rigadoon.
HUGO CHARTERIS, *The Tide Is Right.*
JEROME CHARYN, *The Tar Baby.*
MARC CHOLODENKO, *Mordechai Schamz.*
JOSHUA COHEN, *Witz.*
EMILY HOLMES COLEMAN, *The Shutter of Snow.*
ROBERT COOVER, *A Night at the Movies.*
STANLEY CRAWFORD, *Log of the S.S. The Mrs Unguentine.*
Some Instructions to My Wife.
ROBERT CREELEY, *Collected Prose.*
RENÉ CREVEL, *Putting My Foot in It.*
RALPH CUSACK, *Cadenza.*
SUSAN DAITCH, *L.C.*
Storytown.
NICHOLAS DELBANCO, *The Count of Concord.*
NIGEL DENNIS, *Cards of Identity.*
PETER DIMOCK, *A Short Rhetoric for Leaving the Family.*
ARIEL DORFMAN, *Konfidenz.*
COLEMAN DOWELL, *The Houses of Children.*
Island People.
Too Much Flesh and Jabez.
ARKADII DRAGOMOSHCHENKO, *Dust.*
RIKKI DUCORNET, *The Complete Butcher's Tales.*
The Fountains of Neptune.
The Jade Cabinet.
The One Marvelous Thing.
Phosphor in Dreamland.
The Stain.
The Word "Desire."
WILLIAM EASTLAKE, *The Bamboo Bed.*
Castle Keep.
Lyric of the Circle Heart.
JEAN ECHENOZ, *Chopin's Move.*
STANLEY ELKIN, *A Bad Man.*
Boswell: A Modern Comedy.
Criers and Kibitzers, Kibitzers and Criers.
The Dick Gibson Show.
The Franchiser.
George Mills.
The Living End.
The MacGuffin.
The Magic Kingdom.
Mrs. Ted Bliss.
The Rabbi of Lud.
Van Gogh's Room at Arles.
ANNIE ERNAUX, *Cleaned Out.*
LAUREN FAIRBANKS, *Muzzle Thyself.*
Sister Carrie.
LESLIE A. FIEDLER, *Love and Death in the American Novel.*
JUAN FILLOY, *Op Oloop.*
GUSTAVE FLAUBERT, *Bouvard and Pécuchet.*
KASS FLEISHER, *Talking out of School.*
FORD MADOX FORD, *The March of Literature.*
JON FOSSE, *Aliss at the Fire.*
Melancholy.

CHRISTINE SCHUTT, *Nightwork.*
GAIL SCOTT, *My Paris.*
DAMION SEARLS, *What We Were Doing and Where We Were Going.*
JUNE AKERS SEESE,
Is This What Other Women Feel Too?
What Waiting Really Means.
BERNARD SHARE, *Inish.*
Transit.
AURELIE SHEEHAN,
Jack Kerouac Is Pregnant.
VIKTOR SHKLOVSKY, *Knight's Move.*
A Sentimental Journey: Memoirs 1917–1922.
Energy of Delusion: A Book on Plot.
Literature and Cinematography.
Theory of Prose.
Third Factory.
Zoo, or Letters Not about Love.
CLAUDE SIMON, *The Invitation.*
PIERRE SINIAC, *The Collaborators.*
JOSEF ŠKVORECKÝ, *The Engineer of Human Souls.*
GILBERT SORRENTINO,
Aberration of Starlight.
Blue Pastoral.
Crystal Vision.
Imaginative Qualities of Actual Things.
Mulligan Stew.
Pack of Lies.
Red the Fiend.
The Sky Changes.
Something Said.
Splendide-Hôtel.
Steelwork.
Under the Shadow.
W. M. SPACKMAN,
The Complete Fiction.
ANDRZEJ STASIUK, *Fado.*
GERTRUDE STEIN,
Lucy Church Amiably.
The Making of Americans.
A Novel of Thank You.
LARS SVENDSEN, *A Philosophy of Evil.*
PIOTR SZEWC, *Annihilation.*
GONÇALO M. TAVARES, *Jerusalem.*
LUCIAN DAN TEODOROVICI,
Our Circus Presents . . .
STEFAN THEMERSON, *Hobson's Island.*
The Mystery of the Sardine.
Tom Harris.
JOHN TOOMEY, *Sleepwalker.*
JEAN-PHILIPPE TOUSSAINT,
The Bathroom.
Camera.
Monsieur.
Running Away.
Self-Portrait Abroad.
Television.
DUMITRU TSEPENEAG,
Hotel Europa.
The Necessary Marriage.
Pigeon Post.
Vain Art of the Fugue.
ESTHER TUSQUETS, *Stranded.*

DUBRAVKA UGRESIC,
Lend Me Your Character.
Thank You for Not Reading.
MATI UNT, *Brecht at Night.*
Diary of a Blood Donor.
Things in the Night.
ÁLVARO URIBE AND OLIVIA SEARS, EDS.,
Best of Contemporary Mexican Fiction.
ELOY URROZ, *Friction.*
The Obstacles.
LUISA VALENZUELA, *He Who Searches.*
MARJA-LIISA VARTIO,
The Parson's Widow.
PAUL VERHAEGHEN, *Omega Minor.*
BORIS VIAN, *Heartsnatcher.*
LLORENÇ VILLALONGA, *The Dolls' Room.*
ORNELA VORPSI, *The Country Where No One Ever Dies.*
AUSTRYN WAINHOUSE, *Hedyphagetica.*
PAUL WEST,
Words for a Deaf Daughter & Gala.
CURTIS WHITE,
America's Magic Mountain.
The Idea of Home.
Memories of My Father Watching TV.
Monstrous Possibility: An Invitation to Literary Politics.
Requiem.
DIANE WILLIAMS, *Excitability: Selected Stories.*
Romancer Erector.
DOUGLAS WOOLF, *Wall to Wall.*
Ya! & John-Juan.
JAY WRIGHT, *Polynomials and Pollen.*
The Presentable Art of Reading Absence.
PHILIP WYLIE, *Generation of Vipers.*
MARGUERITE YOUNG,
Angel in the Forest.
Miss MacIntosh, My Darling.
REYOUNG, *Unbabbling.*
VLADO ŽABOT, *The Succubus.*
ZORAN ŽIVKOVIĆ, *Hidden Camera.*
LOUIS ZUKOFSKY, *Collected Fiction.*
SCOTT ZWIREN, *God Head.*